THE KING
FAMILY SAGA

An Amish Honor

AN AMISH ROMANCE

Jennifer Spredemann

Published in Indiana by *Blessed Publishing*.
www.jebspredemann.com

All Scripture quotations are taken from the *King James Version* of the *Holy Bible*.

Cover design by GetCovers ©
Formatting by Polgarus Studio

ISBN: 978-1-940492-84-1 (paperback)
ISBN: 978-1-940492-45-2 (hardcover)
10 9 8 7 6 5 4 3 2 1

BOOKS by JENNIFER SPREDEMANN

AMISH BY ACCIDENT TRILOGY
Englisch on Purpose
Amish by Accident
Christmas in Paradise

AMISH SECRETS SERIES
An Unforgivable Secret - 1
A Secret Encounter - 2
A Secret of the Heart - 3
An Undeniable Secret - 4
A Secret Sacrifice - 5
A Secret of the Soul - 6
A Secret Christmas - 7 (aka 2.5)

AMISH BIBLE ROMANCES
An Amish Reward
An Amish Deception
An Amish Honor
An Amish Blessing
An Amish Betrayal

AMISH COUNTRY BRIDES
The Trespasser
The Heartbreaker
The Charmer
The Drifter
The Giver
The Teacher
The Widower
The Keeper

The Pretender
The Arrangement (releasing 2022 in the Amish
Spring Romance collection)

UNLIKELY SERIES
Unlikely Santa
Unlikely Sweethearts
Unlikely Singing (More Amish Christmas
Miracles collection)

OTHER
The Princess and the Prayer Kapp (Amish Fairy Tale
2-in-1 Collection)
Learning to Love – Saul's Story (Sequel to Chloe's
Revelation – adult novella)
Her Amish Identity (formerly Love Impossible)
An Unexpected Christmas Gift (from the Amish
Christmas Miracles Collection)
The Arrangement (Amish Spring Romance collection)

BOOKS by J.E.B. SPREDEMANN
AMISH GIRLS SERIES
Joanna's Struggle
Danika's Journey
Chloe's Revelation
Susanna's Surprise
Annie's Decision
Abigail's Triumph
Brooke's Quest
Leah's Legacy
A Christmas of Mercy – Amish Girls Holiday

Unofficial Glossary
of Pennsylvania Dutch Words

Ach–Oh

Aldi–Girlfriend

Boppli–Baby

Bruder–Brother

Dat, Daed–Dad

Denki–Thanks

Der Herr–The Lord

Die Heilige Schrift–The Holy Script (Sacred Text, Holy Scriptures, German (Luther) Holy Bible)

Dochder–Daughter

Dummkopp–Dummy

Englischer–A non-Amish person

Ferhoodled–Mixed up, Crazy

Fraa–Woman, Wife

Gott–God

Grossmudder - Grandmother

Gut–Good

Jah–Yes

Kinner–Children

Kinskinner–Grandchildren

Lieb (Liebchen)–Love, My Love

Maed–Girls

Mamm–Mom

Nee–No

Ordnung–Rules of the Amish Community
Schatzi–Sweetheart
Vatter–Father

CHARACTERS IN
AN AMISH HONOR

King Family

Jacob - father

Reuben – Joseph's oldest half-brother

Simeon - Joseph's half-brother

Judah - Joseph's half-brother

Levi - Joseph's half-brother

Zeb - Joseph's half-brother

Gad - Joseph's half-brother

Ash - Joseph's half-brother

Dinah - Joseph's half-sister

Joseph - protagonist

Benjamin – Joseph's younger (full) brother

Dear Reader,

This series is loosely based on stories of actual people who are mentioned in the Bible. These books are not necessarily retellings, although you will find quite a few similarities between the books and their Bible counterparts. I am, in no way, attempting to rewrite the Bible (God has done a fine job with it and He certainly doesn't need my help!) nor am I depicting the true Biblical characters. The characters in my books are portrayed as Amish and there are some things contained in the actual Biblical accounts that simply cannot be included, due to Amish culture and customs. With that said, I hope that you will enjoy this series as it is, but I also hope that it will encourage you to go back and read the *actual* Bible stories themselves. There are so many truths contained in God's Word that we can never even really scratch the surface of its depth. His mercy and grace are beyond measure.

Blessings,
J. Spredemann

PROLOGUE

*J*udah King listened through the door of the room where *Aentie* Rachel—*nee*, now his father's *fraa*—had just given birth. A new *boppli* would be a welcome blessing for all of them. He peeked through a crack in the door, thanks to the midwife leaving it slightly ajar, to see if he could catch a glimpse of the little one.

Dat smiled at his beautiful wife, her brow still wet with perspiration from the labor she'd just endured. "We did it! We have a son, *Lieb*."

Judah frowned. He couldn't remember *Dat* ever looking at his and his brothers' *mamm* that way. It was plain to see that *Dat's* present *fraa* occupied more of his heart than his former wife had.

The rumor flying around the community was that *Dat* had always cared for Rachel, planned to marry her even, until *Grossdawdi* had stepped in and insisted he

1

marry his eldest *dochder* first. Why *Dat*, or anyone, would ever agree to a proposition like that, Judah had no idea. But Judah had never believed those rumors—until now. Perhaps there was an ounce of truth to them.

"A son?" Tears pricked *Aentie* Rachel's eyes.

"*Jah*. He looks right *gut* too." *Dat* was beaming from ear to ear and Judah wondered if that's how Dat had been when he was born. "To share a child with the woman I love more than anything is nearly too much for my heart to handle. How about if we call him Joseph?"

"Joseph sounds like a wonderful *gut* name."

"There's something special about this *bu*, I can feel it." Judah heard the excitement in *Dat's* voice.

"You think *Der Herr* will call him to His service?"

Dat shrugged. "Don't know. I just know he's extra special. We've waited a long time for him, *jah*?"

"Too long."

Judah frowned. Did *Dat* and Rachel mean they'd waited too long since they'd been married or had they meant since they'd met? If it was the latter, then it was almost as if his mother and his siblings hadn't occupied *Dat's* heart much at all. *Nee*, he refused to believe that. *Dat* loved them all. Equally.

"We will be thankful for *Der Herr's* provision. He knows exactly what we need and precisely when we need it. Joseph was born now, at this moment in time, for a purpose that only *Der Herr* knows."

"You are right, husband."

"Would you like to hold him?"

"*Jah*, please." She stretched her arms out to receive the bundle of joy. She gazed down at the wonderful *gut* blessing they'd created together with *Gott's* help. "He's precious. So small."

"What do you think his *breider* and *schweschder* will say?" His father frowned.

"They will love him just as well as we do, I suppose. Do you think we should call them in now?"

"*Nee*. Let's enjoy this sweet one to ourselves just a few moments longer." *Dat* stroked the *boppli's* head. "He is a fine *bu*. A fine *bu*."

"*Jah*, he is."

Judah moved away from the door before the midwife came back and shooed him away. He'd allow his father and Rachel some time alone to dote on their new little one.

He and his brothers had already felt somewhat forgotten since their father had married his new wife. Hopefully, little Joseph wouldn't cause too much disruption to this family.

He frowned. *Was* there something *extra* special about his brand-new baby brother, like his father hinted at? Not that he could tell. He'd have to wait and see.

3

ONE

Seventeen years later...

Joseph shot up from his bed, beads of perspiration trickling down his temples. His heart still raced as though he were being chased by his *vatter's* unruly steer. The shadows from his dream danced in his head, threatening to attack him once again.

He forced his eyelids open, and the sun's rays cleared away the panic that had attempted to overtake him. He looked around his room. His blessed bedroom had never looked so welcoming. He waited a few moments for his heartbeat to return to its normal rhythm.

"Joseph, get out of bed!" His older brother Ash's chiding voice called from the door. "Are you going to sleep all day while the rest of us are chorin'?"

He heard the derision in Ash's tone, something he should be used to by now. "What time is it?"

"Get up and check for yourself, lazy."

Joseph bit back the uncharitable retort that begged to escape his lips. "I'm coming."

He quickly threw on his trousers and work shirt then pulled his suspenders over his chest. He headed downstairs and stopped on the bottom step. His eyes widened as he saw each member of his family already seated at the breakfast table. They wouldn't be happy.

"It's about time," Simeon groused.

Gad shook his head and grunted, not hiding his disdain.

"That's enough!" His father's stern voice held a warning. The boys' untoward behavior would not be tolerated.

His father bowed his head for the silent prayer and the others at the table followed suit. He cleared his throat and picked up his silverware, signaling to the others that his silent prayer had finished and they could now dig in.

"I've got big plans for all of us today."

A collective moan emerged from his brothers.

His father held up his hand to silence them once again. "You will go over to Minister Schwartz's field and harvest tobacco."

Each of his brothers conveyed their disapproval. "All day?"

His father nodded. "If that's how long it takes. With the seven of you working—"

"Seven?" His second oldest brother Simeon frowned, then his head snapped back and met Joseph's eyes with a glare. "What about *him*?"

"I have other plans for Joseph," his father nodded toward him with a half-smile.

"Figures," Levi grumbled.

Dan and Zeb shared a look. "Why does *he* always get out of the hard work?" Dan said.

His father frowned. "He doesn't get out of anything. He works just as hard as you do."

Dan shook his head. "Whatever."

"You will *not* take that tone with me, *Sohn*," his father answered roughly. "You will show respect if you wish to continue to live in this home."

"Sorry, *Dat*." Dan's head hung.

His father turned to him. "Joseph, I have something in the barn for you."

He glanced at his brothers then turned back to *Dat*. "What? What is it?"

"I bought a new mare. A paint. She's yours to take out to the fields. I want you to train her. She will be the driver for your new courting buggy."

Joseph stopped chewing and his mouth dropped open along with each of the brothers'. "A horse? *And a* courting buggy? For me? Thanks, *Dat*!"

He jumped from his chair and gave his father a hug—something his older siblings never did. "I'm going to see her right now."

"Not now, *Sohn*. Finish your breakfast then help your sister with the dishes. They'll be plenty of time to see your new horse and buggy later."

"Yes, *Dat*."

His brothers all sat dumbstruck until Judah managed to speak. "*Dat*, we all had to work for our buggies and paid for them out of our own money. It's not fair that Joseph—"

"It is nobody's business but mine what I choose to give or not. Joseph has worked hard. He has earned it."

Gad snickered, and each one of them shook their heads.

Joseph would never hear the end of this. He was sure of it.

"Now I will hear no more complaints. Do you understand?" Their father eyed each of Joseph's older brothers sternly.

They grumbled, but nobody said another word.

"Boys, hurry along now. Minister Schwartz is expecting you."

"Can't we even finish our breakfast?" Zeb protested.

"Take it with you." His father dismissed them with

his hand, encouraging them to get moving.

Not one of them rose from their chairs.

Ash scowled at him. "It's not *our* fault breakfast was late this morning."

"You should have awoken Joseph sooner." Their father insisted, sipping on his coffee.

His brothers huffed. "We were out doing the chores!" Dan frowned.

"Enough. *Geh*! Head on out now."

Their chairs screeched across the floor loudly as each one of them moved toward the door.

"Have fun playing with your pony today, Joseph." Simeon taunted, purposely bumping his shoulder. Hard.

"Ow!" Joseph rubbed his shoulder.

"*Boppli*." His brother chuckled as he walked out the door.

Joseph exhaled and shook his head, but he was glad to finally have some peace and quiet.

"Why are they always so mean to you, Joey?"

He reached over to his younger brother, Benji, and tousled his hair. "*Ach*, I just ignore them. Don't worry about it."

"But I like you. I think you're nice." The nine-year-old said.

"*Denki*."

"Can I go with you today?"

"It's 'may I' and no you may not. You have school."

"I don't like school much. I'd rather be out workin' with the animals or in the field with you."

"It'll go by fast and you'll be done before you know it. You only have five more years. You just do your best so you can finish on time."

Young Benjamin sighed. "I'll try."

"I'll tell you what. If *Dat* says it's okay, I'll give you a ride to school in my new buggy. You can be the first one to ride in it." He glanced at his father, who dipped his head slightly and winked.

"Really, Joey?"

He smiled and nodded.

"*Denki*. You're the best brother ever."

"I think *you* are." Joseph winked at his brother. "We'd better hurry up if you're to be at school on time."

"Hey, wait a minute. I can't ride in your *courtin'* buggy. I'm not a *maedel*."

Joseph smiled. "It's not *just* for courting, *bruder*."

"You're for sure and certain?"

"*Jah*."

"Okay, then. If you're sure." His steady blue eyes watched his brother.

"I am."

10

"Okay, but just don't make *me* ride with no *maedel*!"

"Why not? Don't you like girls?"

"*Nee*."

Joseph chuckled. "I promise not to pick up any *maed* along the way." Not that he would.

Joseph stood inside the haymow, stacking each bale of hay as his father had instructed.

"How did Benjamin enjoy his buggy ride?" His father asked from the barn floor, his eyes twinkling.

Joseph smiled, remembering how Benji had been so excited when he had allowed him to take the reins for a few minutes. He'd bounced up and down on the plush seat a *gut* minute before they'd even left the yard. "He loved it."

"That *bu* looks up to you." A hint of admiration accompanied his father's words.

"I know. I just hope that I can be a *gut* example to him." The most difficult part was dealing with his older brothers. Many times he'd wanted to speak out, to utter an ill retort that matched their harsh words, but he'd managed to keep a bridle on his tongue. So far.

He needed to pray for his brothers more.

The fact that they loathed him so much bothered him more than he cared to admit. It hurt that they'd never accepted him. He'd always felt like an outsider when it came to his older brothers. He'd always dealt with feelings of inadequacy and inferiority around them. He'd always been the brother that no one invited to go along. They neglected to even acknowledge his presence most times. Unless it was in a negative context, of course.

He remembered something his father had once told him. *God loves you just the way you are. Because someone else can't see your worth doesn't mean that God values you any less. And it is God's thoughts that matter, not anyone else's. You just do your best to live as God wants you to and let Him deal with others.*

He'd tried to live according to his father's advice, but it seemed to be more challenging by the day.

"You are a *gut* example to him, Joseph. I'm proud of the young man you have become. You are very responsible, which is partially why I bought this new rig for you. You have character that your brothers lack."

"*Denki, vatter.* Your words of encouragement mean a lot."

"They are not just words, *Sohn.* They are truth."

Joseph hefted the final bale of hay into the loft,

thankful to be done with this chore. He rubbed his aching muscles. It would be much more efficient if they had one of those conveyer belts like some of the other Amish used. But it had been disallowed in their district. Such conveniences were too worldly.

"Did you take the bales out to the horses yet?" *Dat* asked from the barn floor below.

"Not yet. That was next on my list."

"*Gut*." His father nodded. "I want you to check on the sheep and goats next. Make sure they have plenty to eat. If not, move them on to a different pasture."

"Sure, *Dat*."

"You planning on going to the singing on Sunday?"

Joseph shrugged. "I don't know. Thinking about it."

He usually bowed out of the event just to avoid his brothers. It was bad enough enduring their scorn at home. He didn't want to see what it would be like in public, away from the protection of his father.

"Probably not," he decided.

"I've seen a pretty young *maedel* or two eyeing you at meeting sometimes. Perhaps one of them would like to begin a friendship with you." His father handed him the bridle and grinned. "Now that you have your courting buggy."

Joseph slipped it on his mare, quite a bit easier than he'd expected her to take it. "I'm not interested in any *maed* right now. I'm too young to be thinking about anything serious."

"Perhaps in a few more years you'll change your mind. Still, it wouldn't hurt to go to the singing and join one of the gangs. You can meet new friends, *jah*?"

"Perhaps." He wanted to change the subject as quickly as possible. He surveyed his horse and the cart he'd just hitched up to it. He tossed several bales of hay into the cart as his father raked the loose hay on the ground. "I can do that if you'd like, *Dat*."

"That's alright, *Sohn*. You *chust* take that out to the horses." His father continued his task.

If Joseph admitted it to himself, he sometimes worried about *Dat*. Signs of age had been manifesting themselves for several years now. *Dat* and *Mamm* married later in life and had him and Benjamin in their old age. *Mamm* died when Benji was born and *Dat* had never been the same. As the youngest son, the farm and care for their father would fall on Benji's shoulders. Would he be mature enough to care for their father should he fall ill?

He knew his older brothers—his half-brothers as they continually reminded him—probably wouldn't step up to the plate.

"Joseph," his father called after him.

He abruptly pulled on the reins, bringing his mare to a stop. "*Jah, Dat*?"

"Would you mind going to the young folks gathering anyway? You need to be around young folks your age. It's time."

He wanted to protest, to ask why, but he would do as his father wished. Perhaps his father had been thinking along the same lines he had. Maybe his father was hoping he'd find a mate so there would be someone to care for him in his soon-approaching later years.

Joseph frowned. "*Dat*, are you…okay?" He attempted to keep the worry from his voice.

"*Jah*, fit as a fiddle." *Dat's* eye twinkled, evidencing the truth of his words. "Why do you ask?"

"*Ach*, nothing, I guess." He shrugged. "*Dat*, why do you suppose my *brieder* haven't taken themselves a *fraa* yet?" It seemed their main pleasure in life was making his life miserable.

His father shook his head. "I'm afraid your brothers are taking full advantage of their *rumspringa*. I'm sure they'll settle down. Eventually. But at the rate they're going, *you* might be the one to secure a *fraa* first."

"Me?" He swallowed. He didn't know the first thing about girls and at this point didn't have much desire to learn.

"When the right one comes along, you'll understand." *Dat* smiled. "I knew the moment I saw your mother that I wanted to marry her."

Joseph shrugged, pondering his father's words. "Maybe."

TWO

Joseph knew he would have enjoyed the singing if it hadn't been for his brothers sending him dirty looks half the time. He'd done his best to steer clear of them but they'd still managed to catch his eye from time to time and display their disapproval of his presence.

But he knew that he had just as much right, if not more, to be there as they did. Besides, it was their father who'd insisted he come.

Fortunately, they hadn't been present earlier when their youth group engaged in games of softball and volleyball. He was happy to reacquaint himself with some of his old schoolmates. He'd really been enjoying himself until his brothers showed up. Since they'd left the house earlier than he had, he guessed they'd been up to no good.

Now that the singing was over and folks were

helping themselves to the snacks, Joseph saw it as an opportunity to get out from under their watchful eyes. He'd noticed a few *maedel* looking his way, but he decided that he'd drive home alone tonight. He was in no rush to find himself a *fraa*.

"What are *you* doing here?" Levi sneered as he sidled up to him at the snack table. Joseph was close enough to detect his foul breath.

"*Dat* suggested I come."

"You don't have to worry about finding a *fraa* so you can take care of *Dat*. Our *schweschder* will do that." Simeon took a drink from a small silver flask that Joseph guessed had liquor in it. *Dat* had warned all of them to stay away from liquor.

"What if *she* wants to marry?" Joseph reasoned.

Levi's expression sobered. "No one will want to marry Dinah."

"Why not?"

His brother Simeon came and joined the conversation, rolling his eyes. "Because, *dummkopp*, she already had a man."

Joseph's mouth fell open. "What do you mean? Dinah's been married? How come I never heard this before?"

"Her husband was an idiot." Levi crossed his muscled arms over his chest.

18

"Well, where is he? Why haven't I ever seen him? Or heard about him?" Surely his brothers must be pulling his leg.

Simeon shared a smirk with Levi. "He's long gone. We took care of him."

Joseph's eyes widened. "What do you mean?"

Levi looked at Simeon. "Why are we telling *him* anything?"

"Don't know." Simeon shrugged. "Hey, it's none of your business, *dummkopp*. And don't go asking our sister about it neither. You'll upset her."

Joseph felt a bit of relief as his brothers walked off. Hopefully he wouldn't have to deal with them for the remainder of the evening. Nevertheless, he was eager to return home.

He wondered at what they'd said. Were they simply telling tall tales or was there perhaps a hint of truth to their words? He had never found it peculiar that Dinah didn't go with the young folks, probably due to her age. He'd always just figured that she had in mind to stay an *alt maedel*.

He cast his thoughts aside and determined that he would ask *Dat* later.

All in all, it had been a pretty *gut* evening, he decided. Maybe, just maybe, next time he might ask one of the pretty *maedel's* brothers for permission to ride with their sister.

⌒⌒⌒

"How did your evening go, *Sohn*?"

Joseph glanced at the clock on the wall. It was rare for *Dat* to be up at this late hour. Had he been waiting up for him? Was he worried?

Joseph shrugged. "Pretty *gut*."

"Did you have a *gut* time with the youth folks, then?"

"*Jah. Jah.* Played some volleyball. Talked to some old friends from school." He frowned as he thought of his brothers, who would no doubt return home after a few hours.

"Something is bothering you." How did his father sense these things about him? Was he that easy to read? Or perhaps *Dat* just knew him well.

"*Dat*, the brothers were out drinking and carrying on. Simeon and Levi even told me that Dinah was married before. Can you believe that?"

"*Jah*." His father nodded.

"Why would they make up such ridiculous stories?"

Father frowned. "That's not made up, *Sohn*."

"So, it's true then? They weren't just trying to pull one over on me?"

"*Jah*, it's true."

Joseph frowned. "I don't get it. How come I never

knew about it? Why doesn't anyone ever mention it? What was his name?"

"Those were dark days for our family. It is not something that I wish to speak about, Joseph. Some things are better left unspoken. Your brothers should not have brought it up."

Joseph sensed the frustration in his father's voice.

"Probably 'cause they were drinking."

"*Jah*. Many a foolish thing is spoken when liquor is involved. You must always stay away from it. If your brothers had any sense, they would too. Who knows what other things they've been prattling on about in public." Joseph sensed his father's exasperation and was sorry for bringing it up.

But still, he needed answers to satisfy his curiosity. "Will you not tell me what happened? Please, I am of age. You know I won't share it with anyone. But I do wish to understand my sister better."

"It is a burden you need not bear, *Sohn*."

Joseph frowned. "Do you not trust me, *Dat*?"

"*Nee*, I trust you more than anyone." He sighed. "Okay. But you must never utter a word of this to anyone—not even your *fraa*, should you marry."

"You have my word, *Dat*."

"Your sister was taken advantage of by a man who was not her husband at the time."

Joseph's eyes widened as he digested his father's words. An awful pain clenched down on his heart as though his driving mare were stepping on it. He imagined his sister and what she must have endured. The embarrassment. The shame. The sadness.

"No." Tears sprung to his eyes.

"I'm afraid so."

"Poor Dinah. No wonder she doesn't smile much. What happened to him?"

"Well, he married your sister shortly thereafter. He claimed that he loved her dearly, and I believe he did. It was true that he behaved himself wrongly, but he did try to right his wrongs."

"What happened?"

"Your brothers, Simeon and Levi, were so upset by what he'd done, they took matters into their own hands." He grimaced.

"What do you mean?"

"Well, he fell down a cliff. In reality, I believe your brothers killed him. Arranged it so it would happen in a way that made it look like an accident, so they got away with it. At least, in the eyes of man."

My brothers are murderers? "*Dat*, that's terrible! I—I don't know what to say."

"Now you know why it is never spoken of."

"But what—? How—?" He scratched his head. "Is

that why our family moved when I was little?"

"*Jah*, that is why. It is difficult to gain the respect and trust of others when you have a past reputation like our family's. It is not something folks soon forget."

"Does anyone here know?"

He shook his head. "Not that I know of. Not unless your brothers are shooting their mouths off again."

Would his brothers ever learn any sense? Surely someone could have overheard their conversation at the singing. He prayed it wasn't so, for Dinah's sake.

"*Denki* for telling me, *Dat*. I know it must be hard for you. And for Dinah."

"I'm afraid she has suffered the worst. I feel like I am partly to blame. She wasn't under my protective hand. It wouldn't have happened if I hadn't allowed her to go into town alone."

"*Dat*, I'm sure and certain it wasn't your fault."

"I'm not so certain, *Sohn*. I carry a heavy portion of the blame, the guilt. I keep asking myself why I allowed her to walk to town alone..." His father broke down in tears. "She was my responsibility and I failed her. Her own father failed her."

"I'm sorry, *Dat*. I'm sorry it happened." He patted his father's back in an attempt to comfort him. Aside from when *Mamm* passed away, he'd never seen his father cry. Surely, this was a burden he'd carry with him to the grave.

THREE

Joseph stared at his sister as she worked with her back toward him. Pain clamped down on his heart all over again as he thought of the turmoil she'd gone through. He wished there was something he could do for her, to try to make up for the bad things that had happened in her life. But he knew there was nothing that could wash away the memories that surely haunted her daily.

Dat hadn't wanted him to mention anything, and he wouldn't. But perhaps he could do something for her. Show her some kindness.

"Dinah?"

She kept ironing the shirt she'd been working on. "*Jah*?"

"Is there anything I can help you with?"

She turned around and frowned at him, probably to determine whether he had an ulterior motive. "Sure.

You can get the laundry from the line and bring it in for me."

"Okay." He smiled.

He hurried outside and began removing the laundry from the clotheslines, like he'd seen Dinah and *Mamm* do many times. He carefully placed each garment into the basket until it was overflowing. How much laundry did their family go through?

"It looks like *Dat* has Joseph doing women's work now." One of his brothers harassed him and reached for a shirt. He threw the garment on the ground.

Joseph quickly snatched it up and shook the grass off. "Don't. Dinah just washed these. Do not make more work for her," he warned.

"Back off. I was just teasing you."

Hounding is more like it. He ignored his brother and hefted the basket up to take it inside. He stepped through the door and into the utility room. "Where do you want these?"

Dinah turned now. "*Ach*, just put them in my room. I'll have to get to them tomorrow after breakfast."

"Okay."

He slowed as he approached her room, and proceeded with caution. He'd never been inside it before. Was it okay to enter now?

Dinah had given him permission after all.

He pushed the door open and noticed a distinct difference from his and his brothers' rooms. Dinah's room was nice and neat and it smelled...feminine somehow. He noted the small desk and chair in the corner. His eyes roamed the flowery quilt on her bed. At that moment, an idea popped into his mind.

He quickly deposited the basket of laundry on the floor next to her bed and exited her room. Then he snatched a plastic bag from the kitchen before heading outside. He'd do his best to avoid his brothers' prying eyes.

Joseph went as far away from the house as he could so he could complete his task in silence. He pulled the plastic bag from his pocket. One by one, he gathered different colored flowers and gently placed the delicate beauties into the bag.

With each one that he plucked, he thought of his only sister. She had always been pretty quiet. Of course, with ten males sharing a house with her, even if she *did* speak, she was likely to go unheard.

He knew that feeling very well. Not that he was unheard by his brothers, just ignored or disregarded as though his opinion held no value. But it was different with *Dat*. He always allowed him to speak and he listened to what he had to say. *Mamm* had been that way also. He supposed that Dinah was too, now that he thought about it. Though, he'd never really sat down with her and had a real conversation. Maybe he should change that.

He finished gathering his bouquet when it amounted to a loose fistful. He quickly unbuttoned his shirt and slipped the bag inside, careful not to crush his secret treasure. Surely if his brothers saw it, they'd snatch it from him. And scatter the flowers everywhere. And stomp on them.

He frowned. Why couldn't his older brothers like him? Sure, Judah and Reuben were civil to him most of the time, but he still sensed their air of superiority. As though they merely tolerated him. The other brothers, he was for sure and certain, just hated his guts. Barely endured him because they *had* to. And now that he knew what Simeon and Levi had done, it really disturbed him.

Had his brothers thought they were helping Dinah? Somehow, he couldn't imagine leaving her a shamed, childless widow would benefit her in any way. *Nee,* it only increased her sorrow. How could they believe two wrongs would make a right? Or had they just been prideful and selfish, not wanting their own name to be ruined? Well, *they* sure ruined it alright by their deplorable act of vengeance.

Another thought crossed his mind. If Simeon and

Levi were capable of killing Dinah's husband, who was to say they wouldn't do something like that again?

And they hate me.

He swallowed and loosened the shirt button nearest his throat. *Jah*, he'd have to stay as far away from them as possible.

"Dinah, where do you keep the canning jars?"

She frowned, eyeing him in a strange way. "What do you need a canning jar for?"

"It's a secret."

She stopped her current task—kneading a large bowl of dough at the table—and moved to the sink to wash her hands.

"You don't have to stop. I can get it myself."

Her brow lowered. "You're sure?"

"*Jah*."

She nodded. "There are some extras on the shelf in the basement. They're in a box covered by a towel."

"*Denki*."

"Don't forget the lantern or you won't be able to see." She gestured to the shelf where the extra lanterns were kept.

He found the matches on the shelf as well, turned up the lantern's wick, then watched the flame dance to life. He hurried down the basement stairs and quickly found the box of jars. He took out a pint-sized jar and determined it should work, although he'd need to cut the stems down. But how could he do that without Dinah figuring out what he was up to? He'd have to ask to borrow her scissors. Maybe *Dat* kept some in his desk drawer. *Jah*, he'd check there.

At last, he strode into the kitchen, proudly carrying his bouquet of wildflowers. Dinah had just covered several loaves of bread dough with towels, no doubt to rise. She turned, just as he entered the kitchen.

"These are for you." He grinned, holding out the bouquet.

A confused expression briefly flashed across her face, then tears welled in her eyes. Without warning and without a word, she ran past him and dashed to her bedroom. The door closed behind her with a thud.

His mouth now gaped open and he stared after her, then he stared at the flowers as though they could explain his sister's irrational reaction.

Does she hate flowers? How could anyone hate flowers—especially girls? He was pretty sure that *maed* liked flowers. Usually. Not that he was an expert in knowing what *maed* liked or didn't like. He'd never even courted anyone.

He tiptoed to her room and listened at the door. Still crying. He'd never understand the emotions behind female behavior, he was certain sure.

Should he ask after her? Should he just leave her alone?

"Dinah?" He gently called through the door.

A muffled reply came from the other side of the door. "Go away."

He sighed and tried to figure out what to do with the flowers. He didn't want to throw them away after all the trouble he'd gone through. He could set them on the table, but then they might upset Dinah again. And who knew how his brothers would react to him having picked flowers. He could hear their derision even now. Maybe he'd just take them to his and Benjamin's room. *Jah*, that's what he would do, he decided and headed up the stairs.

"Joseph?"

He looked down at his sister from the top step, still holding the unappreciated jar of flowers. "*Jah*?" He frowned.

"I'm sorry. I'll take the flowers."

Yep, he'd never understand *maed*. "You will? You're sure?"

"*Jah*."

He clomped back down the stairs. "I thought they'd

look pretty in your room on your desk."

"*Denki*." She received the bouquet from his hand. "I…I'm sorry I reacted that way."

"There was a reason, *ain't so*?"

Tears sprung to her eyes again, but instead of running to her room, she simply brushed them away. "Someone gave me flowers before. One time."

He remained quiet in case she wanted to expound on her story.

She shrugged. "He's gone now. I didn't even know him for very long, but I miss him. I always think about what could have been. The life we could have had together."

"Your husband?"

"*Jah*."

"I'm sorry."

"It was a long time ago, but it seems like yesterday. My brothers thought they were protecting my honor." She shook her head. "All they did was make things worse. Do they have any idea how difficult it is to be a woman and not have your own *kinner*? Knowing that you will *never* have your own *bopplin* or husband?"

He did know that children were considered a blessing and most Amish families would welcome as many as the Good Lord gave them.

"Perhaps another man will have you."

"*Nee*. No one would choose me for a *fraa*."

His heart ached at her declaration and the pain behind it. "You could pray."

"Joseph, I've prayed a thousand times. Since I've never received an answer, I assume *that is* my answer. No." She smelled the flowers. "Listen, I'm fine. I have a new normal. I've accepted my lot in life. I don't usually cry about it. Anymore. It's just, the flowers reminded me of him."

"I'm sorry I picked them."

"Joseph, *bruder*, *never* be sorry for doing a kind deed for someone else. Even if the other person doesn't appreciate it, *Der Herr* sees your heart." She leaned over and kissed his cheek. "*Denki*."

She began walking away.

"Dinah?"

"*Jah*?" She turned.

"I would marry you." His cheeks warmed. "I mean, if you weren't my half-sister."

"You, *bruder*, are a sweetheart. You know that?"

He grinned as she walked back to her bedroom with the bouquet of wildflowers. His cheek still felt a bit moist where she'd planted a sisterly kiss. When was the last time anyone had kissed him? Most likely, the last person to kiss him had been *Mamm*.

As Dinah strolled back into the kitchen with a song

on her lips, Joseph decided that *jah*, Dinah would have made a *gut* mother.

Please bless her, Gott.

FOUR

*J*oseph lifted his face as the sun caressed his cheeks. Days like this were his favorite. Just him and *Dat*, with the brothers off somewhere else. Leaving him alone.

They walked along their property—only one of several Dat owned. He'd purchased different plots years ago so he could have ample foliage for the animals, which consisted of horses, cattle, sheep, and goats. Each one served a purpose. The horses were used for work on the farm and for pulling their buggies, the cattle for milk and beef, the sheep for wool and meat, and the goats for their milk.

At that thought, one of *Dat's* favorite verses to quote came to mind. *And thou shalt have goats' milk enough for thy food, for the food of thy household, and for the maintenance for thy maidens.*

With the animals they raised, along with Dinah's

penchant for growing an impressive vegetable garden, and their several fruit trees, they practically lived off the land. Of course, they still shopped at a nearby store or two for other items they required which couldn't be grown in their Midwestern climate.

Like sugar. But Joseph supposed they could even get along without that if need be. His father had always kept a few beehives so they'd have honey year-round. Dinah often used it instead of sugar when she baked bread. The wheat they grew every year was grounded up for flour.

It never ceased to amaze Joseph how *Der Herr* continued to provide for all their needs. It seemed like God had just set everything up in the beginning, put mankind in charge, and let nature take its course. A cycle that reproduced over and over. It was truly a remarkable thought.

It was no wonder his father had wanted so many *kinner*. There was no way he'd be able to tend to this farm all on his own. The men did a lot, but he had no clue how they'd ever get along without Dinah making their meals and tending to their laundry and such. He supposed that *Dat* would need to marry again if their sister ever got a notion to find another husband and begin her own family. But perhaps she was satisfied with what the *Gut* Lord had provided for her. After all,

Joseph had never heard her complain. And up until he'd given her the flowers, he'd never seen her cry.

Jah, she must be content. The thought brought him comfort.

"Remember, Joseph."

Had his father been speaking to him this entire time he'd been lost in his thoughts?

"Sorry, *Dat*. What did you say?"

"I was saying that how you live your life is between you and *Der Herr* and no one else. We must always strive to not just do what is right, but to do better."

"What do you mean, *Dat*?"

"Don't just do what is required. Do more. You will never be sorry for doing more." His father handed him a wrapped candy. "*And whosoever shall compel thee to go a mile, go with him twain.*"

Joseph smiled and popped the soft caramel into his mouth.

His father took his wrapper and deposited both his own and Joseph's into his pocket to throw away later. He reached down and picked up a few pieces of stray garbage that had no doubt been blown into the yard by recent winds. "This is what I mean."

He stared at the fast food wrapper in his father's hand. "Garbage?"

"Yes. Don't be the kind of person that drops garbage

on the ground, taking away from the beauty *Der Herr* intended for us to enjoy. And don't be the kind of person who sees the garbage on the ground and walks by and leaves it there. Be the kind of person who stops and picks the garbage up. In this way, you will leave everywhere you go a better place. In this way, you will be making a difference."

"I don't mind throwing my own trash away, but I don't know how I feel about picking up other people's garbage." He frowned.

"Joseph, we must strive to be like *Der Herr*. He picks up other people's garbage all the time."

"He does?"

"*Jah*, but the garbage *Gott* picks up and discards is called sin. He takes our sins and He removes them from us as far as the east is from the west." *Dat* found a plastic shopping bag on the ground, then deposited the other trash inside. "So when you stop to pick up a piece of trash, remember what *Der Herr* has done for you."

Joseph reached down and retrieved a half-broken empty bottle. He deposited it into his father's trash bag. "I will. *Denki* for teaching me that, *Dat*."

He looked around, amazed at how much prettier the property looked without the garbage present.

"That's what fathers are for." *Dat* smiled, then scratched his beard. "It may seem like a simple thing.

But all the simple, seemingly insignificant things become the big things in life. Like *Der Herr* says in His Word, 'He that is faithful with little will be faithful with much.'"

Joseph nodded.

His father continued, content to offer his sage advice. "Everything we do should reflect our love and commitment to *Gott*. He tells us that in everything we do, we should do it with our whole heart—with unyielding devotion, as to the Lord and not unto man. And that whatsoever we have done unto one of the least of these, we have done it unto Him. *Der Herr* must always be front and center of our lives. Never forget that, *Sohn*."

Joseph briefly wondered if *Dat* had ever had this talk with his older brothers. If so, they hadn't heeded his instruction. *Nee*, they seemed to do the exact opposite.

He determined in his heart that *he* would be different. He would take *Dat's* advice and live according to it as best as he could.

FIVE

"Guess what, *Dat*. I had the most interesting dream." Joseph helped himself to the dish of scrambled eggs in the center of the breakfast table.

He ignored his brothers as they grunted and rolled their eyes.

"Another one?" At least *Dat* seemed interested. He rubbed his beard, sipping on his coffee.

"*Jah*. It was weird." Joseph continued. "It was like I was some prince or something and everyone came and bowed down in front of me."

One of his brothers scoffed. "Oh, yeah, I can see it now. Oh, hail, mighty Joseph!"

"*Jah*, like we'd *ever* bow down to you." Another of his half-brothers chuckled. "Wow! Someone is full of himself."

"It was a dream." Joseph frowned at his brothers' mockery.

41

"Some fantasy in your mind, no doubt." Simeon laughed.

"Joseph, it is best not to speak of these things." His father advised.

"*Jah*, keep your stupid dreams to yourself," Dan said.

"It's not stupid!" Young Benjamin spoke up in his defense. "I like to hear about Joey's dreams."

"Benjamin, *nee*. Do not repeat the words that your brothers say," *Dat* reprimanded, sending disapproving looks to Joseph's older brothers.

"But what do you think it meant, *Dat*?" Joseph persisted.

"Don't mind your dreams, Joseph. They're just dreams, nothing more."

"But I—"

"He said to shut your trap." Dan growled. "Don't you know what that means, *dummkopp*?"

"Joey ain't *dumm*! He's real *schmart*." Benjamin insisted. "And he's nice."

Joseph smiled and winked at his little brother. At least he had one advocate.

"Dan," his father warned.

"He won't shut up. Can't we just eat in peace without him blathering on and on? I'm tired of him and his foolishness."

Benjamin spoke up again. "Joey didn't say nothing wrong. You guys are the ones who say mean stuff all the time."

"Benjamin, just eat your breakfast, *Sohn*." Their father sighed.

❧

After Benjamin had left for school, *Dat* addressed Joseph's brothers.

"I've heard tell that you boys have been out drinking again." Their father's stern eyes frowned at each one of his older brothers.

"Joseph, you little snitch!"

A few curse words spilled out several of his brothers' mouths.

"Enough! You will do Joseph's chores for the rest of the week." Jacob turned to his daughter. "Dinah, your brothers wish to wash the dishes for you tonight as well."

"Ugh!" One of his brothers pounded the table as he forced himself from it. "I hate you, Joseph."

Dinah gasped at her brother's bold words.

"You take that back right now, Dan!" their father demanded.

Dan turned back from the doorway. "No, I won't. It's the truth. Everyone hates him and you know it. You treat him like he's a king and we're his servants. If you had it your way, we *would* all be bowing down to the great and mighty Joseph!"

"That's not true!" Their father insisted.

"*Jah*, it is." Another one of his other brothers spoke up.

"Who just got a new horse? Who got a brand-new saddle? Who just got a brand-new courting buggy?" Dan demanded. "See, I told you. And now, because you've treated him like he's some priceless diamond, he seems to think that we're all going to bow down to him. Well, I certainly won't!"

Joseph watched as Dan stormed out of the house. Shortly thereafter, the rest of the brothers followed suit. How on earth was he going to live in the same house with his brothers if they hated him so much? Maybe it *would* be a *gut* idea to find himself a *fraa* quickly.

SIX

"Joseph, I'd like you to go take this food that Dinah made out to your brothers." *Dat* handed a bulky Igloo container to him and a large bottle of water on a sling.

He eyed it, determining whether he could balance the ice box on his saddle and ride at the same time. *Jah*, he could. The bottle of water would be fine across his torso, although he wasn't used to riding with extra gear.

His brothers had been working on the property *Dat* owned that was furthest from the house. It would take him some time to get there by horse, but he was certain Freckles would do just fine. She'd been a right *gut* horse.

"I wanna go too, Joey!" Benji protested.

Joseph tousled his little brother's hair. "I'm afraid we both won't be able to fit in this saddle. Not if I'm taking this stuff along. Maybe next time, *jah*?"

"Besides," *Dat* interjected, "I have a very special project we need to work on together."

Benjamin's eyes grew like dandelions in spring. "Really, *Dat*? What is it?"

"It's a surprise." *Dat* winked at Joseph. "I'll have to tell you after your *bruder* leaves."

"Well, it looks like you better get going, Joey." Benjamin grinned.

Joseph chuckled, sticking his boot into the stirrup. "You're right. But I want to see what this surprise is all about when I get back."

⁓

Joseph kissed the air to prod Freckles further. He was more than ready to divest himself of the load he carried, although his brothers appeared to be nowhere in sight.

The cattle grazed peacefully on the hills, not even lifting their heads in acknowledgement of his presence.

Had he heard *Dat* wrong? Perhaps he'd gone to the wrong property. He thought back to what he'd been told. No, he was in the right place, for sure and for certain.

The farmer next door raised a hand in greeting. Joseph gently flicked the reins and guided Freckles toward the end of the property line where the man stood, tending his small vegetable patch. It was tiny in comparison to the garden Dinah raised every year and the produce seemed to be half the size. *Jah*, she could probably teach this man a thing or two.

"Have you seen any young men around here?" Joseph asked as he came near the fence that separated the two properties.

The man nodded. "Sure did."

"Do you have any idea where they may have gone?"

"I believe I overheard them talking about a swimming hole or something. They took off in short order. There were two buggies, a car, and a motorcycle."

A car and a motorcycle? Dat would not be happy when he heard about this. His brothers knew better. When would they ever grow up and start acting like responsible adults? They *all* should have joined the church by now and begun their own families. Not that they weren't entitled to a little fun every now and then. But it wasn't just every now and then. Did they realize their uncouth behavior gave the entire family a bad name? Hadn't *Dat* and Dinah already suffered enough ill repute because of their misdeeds? Sometimes, *he* felt like the responsible, older child.

Joseph frowned. "Did you see which way they went?"

The neighbor pointed down the road, opposite the direction Joseph had come. Who knew how long it would be until he found them? But *Dat* had asked him to complete a task and he intended on doing his part. *Dat* would have enough disappointment to deal with concerning his brothers. He certainly did not need to add to his father's burdens.

"*Denki.*"

Joseph turned Freckles around and urged her in the direction the neighbor had pointed. He'd heard of a swimming hole out this way. Hopefully he'd be able to find it before Freckles became too winded. The last thing he desired was to overwork her.

He carefully followed the buggy tracks on the road, searching for any sign of a buggy turning off on a side road. It had been quite a while, but he seemed to remember a swimming hole that *Dat* had taken them all to when he was younger. Could this be the same one? He attempted to recall whether there were any distinguishing features about the place. He remembered a long rope hanging from a big tree that they'd swung out into the middle of the water on. *Jah,* it had been a lot of fun.

Several miles down the road, he noticed where the buggy tracks had turned. There wasn't just one or two sets of tracks though. No, by the look of it, his brothers came down this road quite often.

He continued down the unpaved road for about a mile until he came upon the trail that led to the swimming hole. He heard his brothers' voices hooting and hollering before he could see any of them. Sure enough, there were two buggies and a motorcycle. But there was no car, like the man had mentioned.

He slid off his horse and carried the ice chest and water to where one of the buggies were parked and noticed several beer cans littered among the ground. His brothers wore only their undershorts as they frolicked in the water.

At the sound of his approach, a few of his brothers emerged from the pond.

"Well, well, well. Look who's graced us with his presence." Dan swaggered toward him and bowed at the waist. He'd obviously been drinking. "Your majesty."

"It's a *gut* thing he showed up *after* the girls left." Simeon said.

Ash nudged him in the side. "Shut up, you *dummkopp*. You know he's going to go back and tattle to *Dat*."

Girls? "Were they *Englisch* or Amish?"

Simeon smirked. "Wouldn't you like to know?"

"We're not telling you anything. Chances are, you're already planning what you're going to tell *Dat*," Levi's eyes glowed hot.

Joseph huffed. "What are you doing out here? *Dat* sent you to work with the horses."

Simeon pointed to their buggies, where the horses were still hitched up. "See? We're working with the horses."

Joseph shook his head in disapproval. Who knew how long the poor horses had been standing there hitched up to the buggies. They could have at least freed them and led them to the water for a drink and let them graze on the nearby grass.

"I don't think that's what *Dat* meant." Joseph frowned.

"Oh, so you think you know better than us, huh?" Zeb frowned. "The only thing you know how to do better is snitch."

"There's only one way to deal with a snitch." Levi came near enough to greet him with a holy kiss. He pushed him instead.

Like lightening, fear bolted through Joseph's veins. Surely they wouldn't do their own sibling harm. Maybe he should get going now before they became any more riled up. It seemed like he could never do anything right in his brothers' eyes.

Before he knew it, he was encircled.

"Hey, let's make Joseph's dreams come true." Simeon mocked and bowed down to him. Each of his other brothers followed suit, but it didn't end there.

Maybe sharing his dream with *Dat* in their presence hadn't been the best idea. Joseph held his breath as his brothers took turns unleashing their fury on him. He attempted to block some of the punches, but it seemed futile. He endured blow after blow until he could no longer stand on his feet. It would be a miracle if he survived their wrath.

Pain shot through him, but he was suddenly unaware of what was taking place. Had he blacked out? Was he lying on his back? Something warm trickled from his mouth. He heard muffled voices.

"Let's drive him down to the bridge and throw him into the river."

The river? His heart raced but he couldn't move. Someone grasped his arms and his ankles and he knew he was being moved, but his eyes remained shut.

"*Nee*, not the river." Was that Judah's voice or Reuben's? He couldn't decipher.

But it didn't matter now. All he wanted to do at this moment—all he *could* do—was succumb to the delicious pull of sleep that would make him forget this day. Surely, it had all only been a bad dream.

Jah, a nightmare. That's what it was for sure and certain.

SEVEN

*J*udah stood by, gritting his teeth as one by one his brothers recounted their rehearsed story with the officers. By the officers' tone, foul play was not suspected—unless they were experts in masking their emotions, which they very well might be.

God, I know we did Joseph wrong. I wish I could go back and handle things differently, but it's too late now. Please be with him and protect him. He felt foolish offering a prayer to a God he'd ignored most of his life.

"*Jah*, our brother dropped off our lunch and then he left on his horse. That was the last we saw of him." Judah overheard Simeon's convincing voice.

Their alibi was simple and pretty much fool proof. Unless one of them squealed, which wouldn't happen since they all had a stake in this, the officers wouldn't suspect a thing. And if they did, they wouldn't find anything. His brothers had made sure of that.

They'd returned home in the evening, like they did every day. *Dat* had asked about Joseph and they all recounted the same story—the one Simeon was currently reciting. *Dat* immediately called the police, not even bothering to ask the bishop or any of the other leaders for permission.

"Did you contact your neighbors? Is it possible he might just be at a friend's house?" An officer asked *Dat*.

"My sons have been to every house in our district. No one has seen or heard from him."

Fortunately, *Dat* hadn't suspected anything.

A fuzzy voice came through the officer's radio, and he spoke into it. Judah didn't understand the cop lingo as their communication continued.

The officer stuck the radio back into his belt and looked at *Dat*. "His horse has been found."

"His horse? What about Joseph? Where's my Joseph?" *Dat's* shaking hands splayed in front of him.

"I'm sorry, sir. There's no sign of your son. He seems to have just disappeared." The officer frowned.

His father's chin wavered. "Disappeared? No, it can't be so."

"Could he have run away? Maybe he went off and did the *rumspringa* thing."

"Never! My Joseph would never run away! He'd

never leave his family," *Dat* insisted.

The officer's doubtful look didn't help. "Did he have any enemies?"

"*Nee*. He was a *gut* boy. My Joseph is a *gut* boy. The best."

The officer blew out a breath and nodded. "It seems like we've exhausted our resources. We can put out an APB for a missing persons report. I'll need a photo of your son."

Dat shook his head. "We have no photos."

"Not even one?"

"*Nee*. Amish don't keep graven images."

The officer frowned and Judah stepped forward. "Officer, our Amish group doesn't approve of photographs of our people. We do not take them."

"Well, I'm afraid that without a photograph, a missing persons report would pretty much be useless." The officer sighed.

Out of the corner of his eye, Judah spotted Benjamin running toward their father. He stepped in front of him. "Whoa, there. Wait a minute. You can't go over there. *Dat's* talking to the police."

Benjamin's eyes widened as he looked at the officers then back to Judah. "Where's Joey? Did they find Joey?"

"*Nee*. Nobody knows where he is."

"I want him to come back. I want Joey to come back!"

"Shh…don't make a ruckus. This is serious business."

"But I miss my brother." Benjamin suddenly threw his arms around Judah's waist and cried into his shirt.

Judah patted his shoulder awkwardly. "It's okay. *Gott* knows where he is." Guilt began seeping in.

"Do you think he'll come back?"

"I don't know, Benjamin. The officer said they found his horse."

"Freckles? Where is she?" He peered around him at the livestock barn.

"She's not here yet."

"Is she okay?"

"I don't know." He held his youngest brother at arm's length. "Listen, I need you to go back inside with Dinah. She probably needs your help right now. Why don't you ask her to bring out some drinks for the officers?"

Benjamin nodded, seemingly appeased, and followed Judah's orders.

An hour and a half later, their family sat down to the quietest meal he ever remembered. Only now, he wished Joseph had been there to regale their father with one of his crazy dreams. But he knew that wouldn't ever happen again.

EIGHT

*J*oseph's eyelids attempted to lift open under the intense pressure, but failed. His face must be beyond recognition by the way it felt. A stench rose to his nostrils and caused his stomach to roil. He did his best not to inhale the nasty odor assaulting his senses.

Where am I?

Suddenly a loud beeping noise, like a large commercial vehicle backing up, pierced his ears. In a matter of minutes, he heard a loud tumbling sound, then a crash, and felt heaviness cover him.

He breathed as well as he could with his brother's handkerchief tightened around his mouth. He tried to break free of whatever bound his hands behind his back.

His eyes succeeded in prying open this time, though dull pain accompanied his effort. Darkness surrounded him. His hands brushed against something smooth.

Plastic? I'm inside a plastic bag. A garbage bag?

Had his brothers thought they'd killed him? It would seem so.

The beeping sound came again, and along with it, more heaviness pressed in on him. Then it hit him. *I must be inside a garbage truck!* He wasn't entirely sure how the trash collection process worked, but he was pretty certain that at one point the garbage was crushed beyond recognition.

He attempted to holler, but with the gag around his mouth, his efforts were muffled at best. Completely fruitless. He did his best to not succumb to the fear that threatened to overtake him.

God, please get me out of here.

Because if he didn't get out of here soon, he was quite certain that his older brothers' wishes—for him to be dead—*would* become a reality.

Joseph awakened and realized he was still inside the plastic bag. Praise God for the small air hole at the top. He surely would have suffocated without it. The humidity inside the bag, along with the stench of refuse and lack of fresh air, made it difficult to breathe.

He squirmed and attempted another muffled holler.

Had he heard voices? He strained to listen.

"There. Again. Did you see it?" A male voice said.

"Where?" Another voice asked.

"That black trash bag. It moved. I think there's something in there. Alive."

The voices sounded like they were getting closer. Were they talking about him? *Please, God. Help me.*

"A dog?"

"I don't know. Never can tell in this day and age."

Joseph attempted to kick and thrash about. Perhaps if he made enough racket, they'd turn their attention toward him, if it wasn't already.

"Well, I ain't touchin' it to find out."

Joseph felt something poking his side and he squirmed, attempting to call out.

"Did you hear that? I heard something. I think there's a person inside."

Blessedly, light came pouring through as a man with gloved hands pulled the bag open.

"Oh, my!" The man said. "Are you okay?"

Joseph nodded. The motion increased the pounding in his head.

The man quickly removed the gag from his mouth.

Joseph took in a large gulp of air, not minding the smell of refuse now in the least. He was just thankful to be alive. "Thank you, God!"

The man pulled out a pocket knife and cut the duct tape that had bound his hands and feet.

Joseph had never felt such freedom, despite the fact he was sitting in the midst of a dump, conversing with total strangers. It was funny how complete strangers treated him with more kindness than his own half-brothers.

"Were you in a bar fight or what?" The other guy asked. "You reek of alcohol. And you don't even look old enough to drink." The man chuckled to himself. "Never stopped me either."

His brothers' doing, no doubt.

"*Nee.*" He wouldn't admit that it was his brothers who had instigated his ill fate. "I've never drank alcohol."

The man eyed him doubtfully. "Yeah. And my name is Santy Claus."

"We'll help you out." The other guy—the one that had rescued him—said. He stared at his clothes. "Are you…Amish?"

"Used to be." There was no way he was going back. Not with his brothers out to kill him. He'd rather just let them think they'd accomplished their goal. "Not anymore."

"Do you need a doctor? You look pretty bad."

He probably did. Need a doctor, that is. And if he

appeared half as bad as he felt, he most likely looked like he'd been run over by a semi-truck. "I'll be all right. Besides, I don't have any money."

"That's a bummer, man." The one guy said.

"Where will you stay with no money?"

He hadn't thought that far. At this point, he was just happy to still be breathing. "I have no idea."

"Well, I can give you a ride to the shelter, if you'd like. At least you'll be able to get a meal and a place to spend the night. Probably a hot shower too."

"*Denki*. I mean, uh, thank you. I appreciate that." A hot shower sounded *so* good right now. He could imagine the water beating down on him, massaging his aches and pains. It seemed like Paradise. They didn't have a shower at home, but he'd once used one when they'd stayed at a motel on vacation.

"Not a problem." The guy stuck out his hand. "My name's Steve Maddrey."

Joseph shook his hand. "Jo- uh, Jonah. Jonah Miller...ton."

"Nice to meet you, Jonah Millerton."

"I'm Frank," the other guy said with a shrug.

Joseph nodded. "Thanks again for rescuing me. I probably would have died if you two hadn't come along."

"I'm just glad we could help," Steve said. "My

truck's over in the lot. Frank, why don't you stay here and explain my absence to the boss when he comes by?"

Frank grunted, nodding grudgingly.

NINE

*J*oseph sat at a table across from a man in his mid-fifties, he guessed. It seemed like he'd sent God a thousand 'thank yous' since being rescued from the dump. Now, as the steam from a bowl of hot soup rose to his nostrils, he thanked *Der Herr* once again for His provision.

Jonah eyed the man across from him wondering what his story was.

"I'm Robert Penning, a volunteer here at the Rescue Mission." His brow furrowed as he looked Joseph over.

"I'm uh…Jonah." He set his spoon down.

"It's nice to meet you, Jonah." He offered his hand. "Do you have anyone you'd like to contact?

He thought of his father. Oh, how he wished he could contact him just to let him know he was all right. But if he did, his brothers would know that they hadn't succeeded in getting rid of him. *Dat* would punish them for what they'd done and they'd hate him even more. Next time, he wouldn't be able to escape his brothers' wrath. And there *would* be a next time if they knew he'd survived. It was probably wiser just to lay low.

"No," he said with regret.

"Okay. Maybe you should have a doctor look you over."

"That's not necessary. I don't think anything is broken. I just look and feel terrible." Besides, he had no money.

"Are you sure? We do have a nurse that could do a basic exam. For free."

"I'm fine. Really. I'm sure I just need a bath and some rest."

Robert nodded. "Well, I'll let you finish your meal. Have you been shown where the showers are? Did they assign you a bed already?"

"Yes. Thank you for your kindness to me." Why were total strangers treating him as though he were worth a million dollars when his brothers couldn't even stand to be around him? At least *Dat* had always made him feel special.

"I'll come and talk to you again later after you get settled in, if that's all right with you." Robert stood from the table.

"I would like that."

"Oh yeah. I wanted to mention that we also have a thrift store connected to this building. The items are previously owned, but they are clean. Clothing is free for the residents. If you're in need of some clothes, I'm sure we could find something for you."

Joseph nodded in appreciation.

"Do you have anything other than what you're wearing?"

He glanced down at his clothes—the ones Dinah had painstakingly sewn for him—and frowned. One of his suspenders was now broken, his button-down shirt had been torn and had a button missing, and his broadfall trousers had seen better days. His hat must've been lost when his brothers got ahold of him.

"No. This is all I have."

Well, he had what he was wearing and *Der Herr*. Yes, he still had God. That part had been abundantly evident.

"It looks like you'll need to visit the store then before your shower." Robert smiled. "I'll get you a clothing voucher."

"Thank you." His heart once again filled with gratitude. If he ever became rich, he'd definitely give money to a place like this, he decided.

❦

Joseph perused the rack of clothing and noticed other patrons staring at him. He still smelled of refuse and wore his filthy threads. He'd probably be staring too if he came across someone who looked as wretched as he did. But there was nothing he could do about it at this present moment. All he could do was hurry up and pick out some clothes and get out of there as quickly as possible. A bath never sounded so good.

"May I help you?" An employee approached him.

He frowned at the clothes staring back at him on the rack. "*Jah*. I don't know what size I wear. All my clothes have always been made by my *mamm* or *schwe*—sister."

"Okay, that's no problem. Let's just pick a couple different sizes that look like they might fit and you can try them on." He pointed to a small room with a door that Joseph assumed was a restroom.

Joseph grimaced as he looked down at the soiled clothes he wore. "I don't know if that's such a *gut* idea. I need a bath."

"I'll tell you what." The man smiled. "You can just take them with you and bring back what doesn't fit. How does that sound?"

"*Gut*."

"I'd guess you're about a medium for shirts. Pants, probably thirty-two by thirty-four maybe? Just pick out what you like and we'll check the size." He held up a pair of trousers. "See, the tag's usually right here."

Everyone here seemed so selfless and helpful.

"Thank you."

"That's what I'm here for." He left Joseph to return to the register where a customer waited, then turned back around midway. "You'll probably want to pick out a belt or two as well."

Joseph nodded again in appreciation.

The warm water pelted down with force, covering Joseph's head. The stream that traveled through his hair and into his face was most welcome. This flow of liquid ecstasy was just what the doctor ordered. He'd never known what he'd been missing at home, only having a bathtub for bathing. This, though, felt like rain water straight from Heaven.

It had been a painful chore, peeling out of his clothes. As he surveyed his bruises, he now knew why. *Jah*, his brothers had every intention of killing him.

It was then he realized the truth. He'd never see his brothers or sister again. He'd never see *Dat* again. It was as though he *were* dead to them and they were dead to him.

Why, God?

A sudden inexplicable grief overtook him and he began to sob. His tears mingled with the blessed shower water as they cleansed both his body and soul.

TEN

"Hey, Jonah." Robert appeared at the door of the room Joseph was to be occupying for the evening. "I'm just making the rounds before everyone turns in. Do you need anything? Have any questions?"

"*Jah*, I do." Joseph nodded and Robert stepped into the room.

"May I?" He asked to sit on the bunk next to him.

"Sure. What I don't understand is why you all have been so kind to me." Emotion suddenly overcame Joseph. "I've done nothing to deserve all this."

"Jonah, we love because He first loved us. We like to think that each person that walks through the doors of this place is Jesus. Or at least that they were sent by Him."

"But I'm not Jesus. Why would you do these things for a complete stranger? You don't know anything about me. I could be a really bad person."

"Because Jesus has done so much for me that I can never even begin to repay Him. He knew that I was a filthy sinner, undeserving of His grace, of His forgiveness, of His love. Yet, He died for me anyway. He forgave me anyway. He loved me anyway. I cannot help but live my life to serve Him. He offered me His hands and feet in death. So I want to offer Him *my* hands and feet in life."

"Oh."

"Have *you* received His forgiveness, Jonah?"

He scratched his head. Had he? He knew *about* God and that Jesus died on the cross, but he was unsure about the forgiveness part. He hadn't been baptized into the church yet. Had he ever done anything that needed forgiveness? He knew that his brothers sure had. They needed forgiveness in a big way.

He shrugged. "I don't know. I'm not sure if I have something that I need to be forgiven of."

Robert chuckled. "Everyone needs forgiveness. We're all sinners."

"But I'm Amish—" Oops, he hadn't meant to say that out loud. The last thing he wanted people here to know is that he'd been Amish. "I mean, I have an Amish background."

"And you think that being Amish gives you favor

with God? That you can go to Heaven because of the religion you were raised in?"

"No, I have to be a good person too and abide by the *Ordnung*." Yet, here he was out in the *Englisch* world.

"Jonah, saying that being Amish makes you right with God is like saying that being in a forest makes you a tree. Being part of a religious group—any religious group—will never get *anyone* to Heaven."

Joseph frowned. What did Robert mean? He couldn't mean that his family and friends and acquaintances were headed for hell, could he? Well, maybe his brothers were but... "I'm not sure that I understand. How does a person get to Heaven then?"

"God tells us in the Bible. Do you want to see?"

Did he want to see? What kind of a question was that? Who *wouldn't* want to know how to get to Heaven?

"Yes."

Robert pulled a small black book from his shirt pocket. It was a little smaller than the hymnals their Amish youth used for singings.

"Is that a Bible?" He'd never seen one so small.

"It's just a New Testament." Robert nodded. "The thing with religions is that they are only able to make one conform on the outside. But those good works are just acts—deeds to be seen by man. It is only God who can change the heart and make a new man. It has to work from the inside out. And that can *only* happen when Christ enters a man's heart."

Joseph nodded. It made sense. He knew a lot of people who were baptized Amish and acted, well, like his brothers. They didn't have the compassion that these people showed.

"And just remember that people that *do* have Christ in their lives are not going to be perfect. Our sins have been erased, but our sin nature hasn't. Everyone is a work in progress. But you *should* know them by their fruit."

Robert opened his small Bible. "I'm going to read from the book of Romans, starting with chapter three. *For all have sinned and come short of the glory of God.* A few verses up, it also says *There is none righteous; no, not one.*"

He looked at Joseph. "So, if no one is righteous and all have sinned, that pretty much puts everyone in the same boat, right? Amish, Catholic, Jewish, Buddhist, Protestant, Baptist, Mormon, none of those titles matter. The Bible doesn't even mention them here. All are in a mess as far as God is concerned. All have come short of His glory."

Joseph frowned. Robert's words, or God's Words, didn't paint a very good picture. "Well, then *who* can go to Heaven? Who can escape Hell?"

"That's a good question. You know, there were people in the Bible who wanted to know too. Jesus told Nicodemus, '*Except a man be born again, he cannot see the kingdom of God.*' He explained to Nicodemus how much God loved the world, enough to send Jesus to die for us. He promised that *whosoever believeth in him should not perish but have everlasting life.* And when the Philippian jailor asked Paul and Silas what he must do to be saved, they told him to *believe on the Lord Jesus Christ, and thou shalt be saved.*"

"So, that's it? Just believe?"

"Well, the Bible also says that even the devils believe and tremble, so I'm guessing the difference is in where your heart lies. The devils and probably most people living today have a basic head knowledge of Jesus Christ and who He is. Just knowing and believing that something happened doesn't mean anything. You also have to receive Him."

He flipped a few pages in his Bible. "I think that's why Paul goes on to clarify in Romans. Here, let me read it to you. *That if thou shalt confess with thy mouth the Lord Jesus, and shalt believe in thine heart that God hath raised him from the dead, thou shalt be saved. For with the heart man believeth unto righteousness; and with the mouth confession is made unto salvation.*"

Joseph rubbed his chin. "I think I get it."

"Think of it this way, Jonah. Remember when that really bad hurricane hit the gulf coast and all of those cities and towns were covered in water?"

Joseph nodded. He remembered it well. It had been plastered on every newspaper he'd seen. They'd even prayed for the victims.

He continued. "Well, imagine if you were sitting on top of your house and I came by with my boat. You see my boat and you know that it's there and that it's available to you. I call to you on your rooftop telling you that I can save you, but you'll need to get in the boat.

"You tell me that you appreciate my offer and you do believe that I can save you, that I and my boat are capable. But instead of getting in the boat, you decide that you'll figure out your own way to get to safety or that you'll wait until the water rises higher. After all, your friends are still sitting on the rooftops of their houses. They didn't accept my offer either and they seem to be fine. So you never accept my offer."

"I'd be a fool."

Robert nodded. "In order to benefit from my boat, to be saved, you'd have to receive my gift—my offer—personally. Just believing is not enough. In order to benefit from the cross, to be saved, you have to accept

Christ's gift—His offer—personally. Does that make sense?"

"Yes, that makes perfect sense." Joseph smiled. "What do I need to do to receive Him?"

"Just ask Him and believe in your heart, like the Bible says in the verses we just read."

"Okay." Joseph bowed his head and prayed silently, the way he'd always seen his father do. *Gott, please save me. Cleanse me of my sins. Take me to Heaven someday. Denki. Amen.*

Robert bowed his head as well.

Joseph shifted off the bed a bit to let Robert know he was finished, but Robert kept his head bowed for a while. Joseph waited a little then cleared his throat. Eventually, Robert looked up with a grin on his face and tears in his eyes. *He was crying?*

"Sorry. I tend to get a little emotional when a new soul trusts Christ. Do you realize that the angels are rejoicing in God's presence *right now* because you just accepted Christ as your Saviour?"

"What?"

Robert turned again to a passage in his Bible. *"I say unto you, that likewise joy shall be in heaven over one sinner that repenteth, more than over ninety and nine just persons, which need no repentance.* And a few verses down Jesus states, *Likewise, I say unto you, there is joy in the presence of the angels of God over one sinner that repenteth."*

"Wow! That's wonderful *gut*."

"It is, isn't it? Praise God." Robert turned to him. "So, do you have any *more* questions?"

"*Nee*, no, I don't think so. I'm going to Heaven now, *ain't so*?"

"Yep, you've got God's promise on that. You are now sealed until the day of redemption and nothing can snatch you from His hand."

"Sealed?" The term was unfamiliar to him.

"Yep. When you trust Christ, the Holy Spirit comes to live inside you. You belong to God. You are His child. He *never* disowns His own."

Joseph frowned. "Not that I would, but what if someone disowned Him?"

"Good question. Which is why I believe God put those verses in the Bible. They are very comforting. There's nothing I can do to lose what God has given me. I'm not the keeper, He is. Even if I wander away, I am still His child. It is Christ and *His* power that keep me saved. I'm not strong enough to extract myself from God's hand. No one is. *For I know whom I have believed and am persuaded that he is able to keep that which I've committed unto him against that day.* See, God does the saving *and* God does the keeping."

Joseph shook his head. "That's…amazing."

"Yes, it is. God is so so good." He scratched his chin. "Now, we *can* choose to disobey our Heavenly Father. If we do that, though, we will be corrected. Just like our earthly fathers are supposed to do."

Joseph nodded. "What if I mess up? What if I do something I'm not supposed to, not even knowing?"

"Well, God is not out to punish His children. He loves us. He wants us to have joy and peace. But He knows that sin will only bring us heartache, so He gently guides us along the right path so we can avoid all the pain and heartbreak. He wants us to lean on Him and trust Him fully with our lives. We need not fear His wrath."

"How do I know what He wants me to do?"

"Read His Word and ask Him to show you. He will." He handed the small Bible to Joseph. "Take this. Read it every day and you will find God's will for your life."

"You're sure?"

"Yep. I can get another one."

Joseph held the small book in his hands and caressed it as though he'd been given a treasure. "*Denki*. Thank you very much. I'll read it."

"You do that, Jonah. And I'll be praying for you."

"Thank you."

"I have a feeling God is going to use you to do great

things." Robert squeezed his shoulder.

"You think so? I have so little. And I'm nobody."

"That's exactly why He *can* use you. He gives grace to the humble. Stay humble, Jonah, and you'll see God do mighty things through you."

ELEVEN

Joseph now lay on the twin bunk provided by the local rescue mission. Once again, He thanked God above that places like this existed. He didn't even want to imagine where he would be right now if Steve hadn't directed him here. He had been correct about the shower and hot meal, but he'd received so much more than just that. What a blessing. He'd be eternally grateful.

He never even could have dreamed—okay, maybe he *could* have dreamed it—himself in a circumstance such as this, but alas, here he was.

A longing for home—for *Dat*, for Benjamin, for Dinah—caused an ache in his heart even greater than his physical injuries. The thought of never seeing any of them again brought him to tears once more.

What would he do without them?

What would *they* do without him? How would they

respond to his absence? Would *Dat* mourn for him? Surely he would. They'd had a special bond, he and *Dat*. This would be difficult for *Dat* to endure, for sure. Especially after losing *Mamm*.

Gott, please be with them. And me.

He couldn't believe his brothers hated him enough to kill him! As long as he could remember, they'd always reminded him that he was their *half*-brother. Was he so intolerable that they felt the need to do away with him? Being here evidenced that fact more than anything else. The rejection stung.

Were they hoping to get *Dat's* property? Was that what they were hoping for? Because if they were, Benjamin should beware. If they'd already killed a man and were willing to kill their own brother, who knows what kind of evil they were capable of.

Gott, please protect Benji. And let my family find You. They need you, Lord.

"Well," Robert said, patting Joseph's back, "I hate to see you go, brother. You sure you don't want to take advantage of those HSE courses and get your diploma? You're welcome to stick around longer."

"Yeah. I need to start working. Thanks for introducing me to Mr. Hayes."

"Not a problem. I hope it goes well for you." He pointed to the backpack the rescue mission had furnished Joseph with. "I wrote my name and phone number in the back of the Bible for you. If you ever need anything or just want to talk, I'll be here. That is, unless the Lord calls me home."

Joseph quirked a brow. "You live here?"

"Yep."

"You don't have a family of your own?"

He released a heavy sigh. "I did. I ruined it, though. I used to be into drugs and some really bad stuff before God saved me. I messed up a lot of things in my life— things that were meant to be blessings. I lost it all. But I found Jesus. Or, I should say, Jesus found me." He smiled.

"Where is your family? Did they die?"

"No, they're still alive. They live out in California somewhere, I think. My wife remarried and she seems happy now."

Joseph noticed a shimmer in Robert's eyes. "I'm sorry."

"You don't need to be. We all make our own choices and we've got to live through them. I just hope that you will make wiser choices with your life than I did."

Joseph nodded. "With God's help."

"Yep. I wish I'd known Him sooner, but it seems like it takes a special set of circumstances for a man to reach out to God. Some of us have to come to the end of our rope before we see how much we need Him."

"I know what you mean. I never thought I'd end up here."

"Jonah, this isn't the end. This is just the beginning. Keep your eyes open and you'll be amazed to see how God works in your life."

"Really?" A sudden excitement welled within Joseph's soul. Did God really have his life planned out? Would He really direct his steps? Surely, there were good things to come!

"You just keep your nose in the Book and fix your eyes on Jesus."

"I'll do my best."

TWELVE

"**W**ell, this is the new place where we'll be working for the next few weeks." Mr. Hayes grinned with pride. "What do you think, Jonah?"

Joseph surveyed the land before him. Row after row of corn stretched out as far as his eye could see. Just how many acres of land did this farmer own? *Wow!*

Out of all the places they'd worked over the last two years, this one surely took the cake.

"It's amazing. I don't think I've ever met anyone who owned this much land." Joseph shook his head.

"Chances are, you won't be meeting the owner of the Cornucopia Plantation either. He's a busy man and he doesn't spend a lot of time out in the fields. That's why we were hired."

"Have *you* met him?" Joseph asked his boss.

"Sure. He's a pretty nice guy."

Joseph would love to have an opportunity to talk to the man and learn the secret of his success. Did he work for all this or had he inherited it? Either way, it was plain to see that God had prospered him.

He couldn't complain about his own circumstances, though. God had been very good to him. He saved up what he could, but getting ahead almost seemed like a pipe dream. He hoped to someday have more than the small apartment he inhabited now. One day, God willing, he'd like to have his own place, start a family of his own.

He'd thought long and hard about going back to the Amish, possibly finding another district to join. But he knew how things worked in the Amish culture. Without a doubt, his family would discover that he was Amish again. His brothers would know he was still alive and well. If they didn't find out through the leadership, or a letter from a friend or relative, they'd surely read it in The Budget. And that was something that he couldn't chance.

If he ever did have a family of his own, he wondered what it would look like. Would he marry an *Englischer?* Most likely. But there seemed to be so many differences in culture. He often felt like he was doing things backwards or the wrong way. Would an *Englisch* woman even be interested in an ill-mannered former-Amish man? He highly doubted it.

He thought of the young women his age that he'd seen at church. For the life of him, he could never picture himself with one of them. Not that they weren't nice. Or attractive. He just felt too different. Maybe not on the outside, but on the inside for sure.

But if he wasn't suitable for any of the women at church, who would he be compatible with? He couldn't marry an unbeliever. That would go against God's will for his life.

He sighed. Maybe it was better if he just didn't concern himself with marriage. If God wanted him to marry, surely He'd let him know.

Wouldn't He?

The sun burned hot in the early August sky and Joseph tipped his hat to shade his face. This cowboy hat he'd worn for the last couple of years seemed quite a bit sturdier than the straw hat he'd worn when he was Amish, but it didn't let as much breeze through.

He glanced down at his *Englisch* clothing and briefly wondered if his Amish family would even recognize him now. Probably not, with the combination of his clothing, hat, and the scruff he wore on his face.

He felt a bit strange wearing a trimmed beard because he wasn't married, but he constantly reminded himself that he was in the *Englisch* world now and the rules were different. Women didn't assume you were married just because you sported facial hair. Besides, several of his coworkers had commented on it, saying it made him look like a man.

Had he grown into a man over the last couple of years? He knew that he'd changed quite a bit—on the outside, at least. But he knew deep down in his heart that there would always be a part of him that remained Amish. It was his heritage, what his father and mother had intended for him. But perhaps God intended something else.

One thing he savored in the *Englisch* life was the respect of his peers. That was something he didn't think he'd ever get at home—even if he did marry and have his own *kinner*. No, he never would have garnered the same respect from his older brothers.

"You're staring."

Joseph looked up to see a pretty face. A young woman near his own age wore a cowboy hat with a blonde braid to one side which nearly hung down to her waist. She sat atop a horse.

"Oh, yeah. Um…it seems like forever since I've ridden a horse. I must've been daydreaming."

"I saw you over there with the guys. You're different, aren't you?"

She'd noticed? Joseph frowned. Being different had gotten him into trouble in the past. Did she know by simply looking at him that he was Amish? "What do you mean?"

"Well, you're usually the one to offer drinks to the others. Every time I see them smoking cigarettes and drinking after work, you're off doing something else."

"Yeah. My *vat*—my dad taught me to stay away from the temptations of the devil." He could've kicked himself. He'd been doing his best to overcome his Amish accent and speech, but sometimes it just slipped out.

"It sounds like your father was a wise man. You must take after him."

"Thank you. I'll take that as a compliment."

She smiled. "I meant it as a compliment."

"Oh. Thank you."

She laughed. "You already said that."

He chuckled at himself. "Yeah, I guess I did, didn't I?"

"What's your name?"

"It's Jonah Millerton."

"Well, Jonah Millerton. I'm pleased to make your acquaintance." She held out her hand to shake. It was dainty but strong. "I'm Azalea."

"Azalea?" He grinned. Why did that name sound so familiar?

"Hey, don't judge me. My parents were kind of hippies."

He laughed, although he was unfamiliar with the term 'hippie'. "Okay, I won't. I actually like your name. It's different."

"A little more unique than Jonah Millerton, huh?"

He shrugged. "A little. Hey, isn't azalea a type of flower?"

"Yes, it is."

"Hmm…if I recall correctly, it's beautiful but deadly." He grinned.

She arched a brow and smirked. "Yep, that's right."

"Seems fitting." He winked.

"So, are you saying I'm deadly?" She feigned offense.

"I don't know, are you?" He kicked a clod of dirt with his boot.

"Maybe." Her upper body seemed to sashay when she said the word.

"Well, you're certainly beautiful." Shoot, maybe he shouldn't have said that. But it was too late to take it back now.

Her cheeks exploded into a beautiful pink and she tugged her bottom lip between her teeth.

"Well, I better get going. My dad will be expecting me back soon." She tilted the tip of her cowboy hat down with her hand, then took off faster than he'd ever seen any woman ride.

He watched after her.

"Don't go getting any ideas." His coworker, Michael, warned as he came up beside him, interrupting his train of thought.

"About?" His brow rose.

"About the pretty little filly." He pointed at the cloud of dust that hung in the air. "The owner's *daughter*."

"Azalea is the heir to the Cornucopia Plantation?"

"The one and only."

"I had no idea."

"Yeah, well. Now you know. Keep your distance."

"Why? She seemed really nice."

"Nice? Most men aren't after her because she's nice." He lifted his eyebrows twice in quick succession.

Anger flared at Michael's assumption. "Well, I'm not most men."

"Mm…hm. And my name's not Michael Swanson." He punched Joseph's shoulder. "Besides, the boss said our work crew's going to be moving on before long. So don't even think about putting down roots."

Joseph frowned as Michael sauntered off.

He looked back in the direction Azalea had ridden. There was something special about her, although he wasn't exactly sure what it was. Was this what *Dat* had meant when he said he would know the one when he met her? Is this how *Dat* had felt when he'd met *Mamm*? But *Dat* hadn't married *Mamm* right away, he'd married her sister instead. Why?

Now he wished he'd asked *Dat* more questions when he was at home. He'd never known the reason *Dat* married his half-brothers' *mamm* first. The only time he'd ever asked about it, he'd been younger and met with the 'you're too young to understand' answer. Which, at the time, that was probably the truth.

If only *Dat* were here right now. If only he could procure his advice.

At this point, he was unsure if Azalea was even a believer. Maybe he *should* steer clear of her as Michael had suggested. But if he did, he'd never find out whether she was a believer or not. He at least needed to know that much.

Gott, help me to be strong for You. Guide my path in the way You would have me go.

THIRTEEN

*J*ust a few more rows and Joseph would be finished with the work he'd hoped to get done before lunch. He enjoyed the views from sitting so high up. He'd never used any farm vehicles before he got hired on by Mr. Hayes. They really cut out a lot of the manual labor on a farm. Things that would have taken his family days to accomplish could be done in several hours.

"Hi, Jonah." A female voice called loudly from the outside of the farm vehicle.

He twisted to see the owner's daughter astride the same horse he'd seen her on the other day. Another horse trailed behind, devoid of its rider. He killed the engine of the farm vehicle. "Azalea, right?"

"You remembered." Her pretty smile matched the rest of her.

How could I forget? You're almost all I've thought about...

91

He realized she was staring at him, probably waiting for some kind of response. "Yes, I did."

"You about to take a break for lunch?"

He nodded.

She looked around at the other workers then her gaze settled on him again. "Are you allowed to leave?"

He shrugged. "As long as I get back to work when it's time."

"I'd like to show you something." Her eyes sparkled.

"What?" She wanted him to go somewhere with her? She desired to spend time with him? He grinned like a fool.

"It's a secret."

A secret, now *that* was intriguing.

"I...don't know if it's a good idea." He looked around at the other guys on the crew, who were now breaking for lunch.

"Come on. I even brought you a horse." She beckoned. "You said you know how to ride, correct?"

"Yeah, I know how to ride." Although it had been a while, he didn't think it was something he'd ever forget. Along with his many memories of home. He shrugged. "Well, okay. If you're going to twist my arm."

He dismounted the farm vehicle, deciding he'd finish the job after he returned from lunch. After all, it wasn't that important at the moment. It also wasn't every day he received an invitation from a pretty young woman.

"Let me grab my lunchbox from the truck."

"You don't need to. I brought enough for both of us." She patted the knapsack behind her.

Joseph grinned. She brought him lunch? "Okay."

He slipped his foot into the stirrup and easily swung up into the saddle.

"You've done that a time or two, huh?" She smiled.

"Yeah, once or twice." He winked, then gently prodded the horse with his boot. "Where are we going?"

"Follow me." She nudged her horse, then took off at a gallop.

Joseph smiled and shook his head. He loved her spunk. "Hee ya!" He called to his horse to chase after her. This was turning into a fun lunch hour.

Nearly ten minutes later, they crested a small hill. When Joseph looked down, he couldn't believe the beauty before him. A thicket of trees surrounded a shining aqua lake. He never would have guessed this hidden gem existed, had he not seen it with his own eyes.

Azalea kissed to her horse, maneuvering around trees until they came upon the lake's bank.

Joseph stared out at the sparkling blue-green water.

The lack of breeze rippling the small lake created a pristine image—a perfect reflection of the surrounding trees. "Wow, this is…amazing."

"Yeah, it's my little secret place." She smiled and winked. "So don't tell anyone."

He zipped his lips with his thumb and forefinger. "Your secret's safe with me."

She dismounted her horse and led it to the lake for refreshment, allowing the creature to consume its fill of water, then wrapped the reins around a tree branch. Joseph followed suit.

"You hungry?" She released the knapsack from her saddle, along with a lap blanket.

"Starving."

She spread the blanket out on the ground under the shade of the trees, then sat down. She patted the space next to her. "Come eat."

He sat down beside her and received a sandwich from her outstretched hand. "Thank you."

"You're welcome. I hope you like chicken salad."

"I don't think I've ever had it before."

"Really?"

He nodded.

She glanced down at the sandwich in her hand. "Do you mind if I pray?"

"*You* want to pray?" He frowned. He wasn't

accustomed to women praying. As a matter of fact, he couldn't remember a time when *Mamm* had prayed on her own. Of course, that didn't mean she hadn't, he just never saw her.

"Why do you say it that way?" Her brow lowered. "Unless…do you want to pray? You're more than welcome to."

He'd noticed since he'd entered the *Englisch* world that nearly everyone prayed aloud. Did Azalea want him to pray in this manner as well? Wasn't one supposed to go into their closet and pray? They were not to stand on the street corners and make an open show to be seen by men. Of course, this was hardly a street corner. This *Englisch* lifestyle held peculiar customs indeed.

"Do you mean out loud?" He voiced his thoughts.

"Yeah." She clarified.

"Well, I don't really…I mean, I usually…I'm more comfortable praying to myself."

She laughed. "You pray to yourself?"

He guessed by the gleam in her eye that she was teasing him. "No, I meant silently. I pray to God. Who do *you* pray to?"

"God. Jesus." She smiled. "Would you like me to pray then?"

He nodded. "Sure, if you'd like."

They both bowed their heads and she prayed aloud. "Dear Lord, thank You for this food You've provided for our nourishment. And thank You for allowing Jonah and I to spend some time together today. May our thoughts, actions, and speech be pleasing to you. In Jesus' name, Amen."

Perhaps she was a believer. This day just kept getting better. He suppressed another smile.

Joseph took a bite of his sandwich and groaned when it met with his taste buds. "This is so good," he mumbled around his mouthful of food.

She playfully shook her finger at him. "Didn't your mother ever teach you manners? You're not supposed to be talking with your mouth full."

"Manners? No. My mother died when I was young."

Azalea frowned. "Oh, I'm sorry. My mother passed away too."

"When?"

"About two and a half years ago. It's just me and Dad now." She offered him some potato chips and pulled out a container of dip.

"You don't have any brothers?" He took a small handful of chips and popped one into his mouth.

"Nope. I'm an only child. My mom's pregnancy and my birth were pretty rough on her. After I was born, she got pregnant twice but lost both babies to miscarriage.

So I guess I was somewhat of a miracle baby."

"A miracle indeed." He winked. He'd never really flirted or spent much time with a *maedel* before, so he found this time with Azalea rather fascinating.

"How about you? Any siblings?"

He nodded, then looked away.

"I'm sorry. Is that a sore spot?"

"Yeah. I'd rather not talk about it."

"Okay, that's fine. We don't have to." She pulled out a container of watermelon. "Want some?"

He smiled and nodded. "This is a good lunch."

"Thanks. I'd hoped you'd like it." She ate a few forkfuls of watermelon. "You want to go swimming when we're done?"

"Swimming? I'm not really dressed for that sort of thing."

"Why don't you bring some swim trunks tomorrow and we can go in the water?"

The thought of swimming with a pretty young woman caused his temperature to raise a few notches. He swallowed. "Okay."

As of now, he had no swim trunks but he would buy some to have an opportunity to swim in the lake with Azalea.

"So, what are your plans, Jonah? What do you want to do with your life?"

"I don't know exactly. I haven't really thought much about it."

"No plans for college? Do you plan to work with this crew your whole life? Start your own business?"

"*Ach*, so many questions." He laughed.

"Well, when I tell my dad about the guy I'm interested in, he's going to want to know everything about you."

His brow shot up. "You're interested in me?"

She nodded. "I thought it was obvious."

"Sometimes men don't *get* what's obvious." He smiled. "Okay. School. Um, no. I'm not planning to go to college." Should he mention he'd only completed eight grades? "I grew up Amish, so I only had school until grade eight."

Her eyes grew wide. "You mean, you didn't even finish high school?"

"No high school at all. After we finish school, we basically go to work, learn a trade." He shrugged.

"Oh." She frowned.

"Is that a terrible thing?" To him, it was normal. But he wasn't living in an Amish community anymore. It seemed he had so little in common with *Englischers*, comparatively speaking.

"Well, not to me. But it is where my dad is concerned. Have you ever thought about getting your GED?"

"What's that?"

"It's a test that people take that is basically equivalent to a high school diploma."

Was that the same thing Robert at the Rescue Mission had told him about? No, it had a different name although he couldn't rightly remember what it was at the moment. "You mean that people can just take a test instead of going to high school?"

"Well, kind of. You'd have to study hard because it covers most of what you'd learn in high school. Most people study for several months before they take the test. It's not that simple."

"And high school takes four years?"

She nodded. "That's right."

"It wonders me why everyone doesn't do it that way instead of spending four years of their life in school."

"Huh, I never thought of it that way. I think a lot of parents probably want their children to have the experience of high school—you know—sports, dances, games, that kind of stuff. But high school is mandatory for most of the population, at least up to a certain age. I guess the Amish must be excluded in that law.

"A GED is sometimes looked upon by some people as not being as good as actually attending high school. At least, that *used* to be the stigma. I think it's probably a little more accepted now with the increase in homeschooling and independent study programs."

He had no idea what the word 'stigma' meant, had never even heard the word, but he understood the gist of what she was saying. Maybe that was one of the words *Englisch* folks learned in high school, he mused.

"Would you want to take it? I could help you study if you did."

He frowned. He'd always been taught that higher education held the temptation of one becoming *hochmut*—proud. He didn't wish to become proud. God honored humility. *God resisteth the proud but giveth grace to the humble.* He did admit that spending more time with Azalea was appealing, though. "Why would I take it?"

"It can probably help you get better-paying jobs. It looks better on a resume."

"What's a resume?"

"It's a piece of paper that employers usually require that lists all your educational and work experience. It'll help you get jobs. A lot of employers will ask for your resume if you're going to work for them."

"Wow. It sounds like I have a lot to learn. How'd you get so smart?"

She shrugged. "I went to school."

Yet Azalea didn't seem to be lifted up by pride. Not to him, anyway. "*Jah*, then. Maybe I should take that test."

She smiled. "I can get all the info on it for you if you'd like. Do you have a library card?"

"No."

"Okay, here's what we'll do. Are you free after work today?"

"Michael usually gives me a ride home."

"You don't have a car?"

"No license."

"Aye, Jonah. Okay. First, let's work on getting you a driver's license. Then, we can see about studying for the GED."

He frowned. "I don't know if I'll have time for all that. Michael said the crew will be moving on in a few weeks."

"Do you have to go with them? I could ask my dad to hire you on full time."

He smiled. "That's nice of you to offer, but I don't have a car, remember? I don't know how I'd get from here to home and back. I'm kind of at the mercy of Michael."

She frowned. "You'll keep in touch then, right? Give me your phone number."

"I don't have one."

"You don't have a phone *either*?" Her voice screeched. "How do you even live, Jonah?"

He chuckled. "I live simply. A phone is extra cost

and I really don't have anyone to call."

"Well, you do now." She winked. "So, tell me what it was like growing up Amish."

He shrugged. "Normal for me, I guess. I didn't really know any other way. We used a horse and buggy for transportation. I probably rode my first horse when I was about two. With *Dat's* help, of course."

"Is it true that you guys don't have electricity?"

"Yep."

"So, what did you do in the summertime? You had no air conditioning, right?"

"In the evening, we'd open the windows to let the nice breeze in. We'd leave them open until morning before it started getting warm, then we closed them up. Sometimes it was even a little chilly in the mornings. Then, if the house stayed closed, it usually kept cool. You'd be surprised."

"But don't the Amish use woodstoves to cook on?"

"We had a summer kitchen. In the summertime, *Mamm* or my sister would cook out there."

"Was it in a separate building or a separate room?"

"The Amish do it either way. It's best if it's in a completely separate building, though. That's how ours was."

"So, did you just move the stove back and forth then?"

"We had two, but some only have one and move it. There are usually two separate chimneys, so they just connect the pipes. I'm glad we had two separate ones, though, because those things are *very* heavy and a pain to move."

"I can imagine."

"Enough about me. Tell me about you."

She shrugged. "Not much to tell, really."

"What do you do all day?"

"Whatever I want. I'm trying to hone my photography skills, so I take a lot of photos."

"Really? Of what?"

She shrugged. "You know, this and that. Flowers, horses, sunsets... you."

His brow shot up. "*Me?*"

Her cheeks blossomed with color. "Uh...yeah."

"Why?"

Her eyes surveyed him from head to toe and she lifted a brow. "Why not? Jonah, you're..."

He shook his head. "Oh, no. You go ahead and finish that sentence. I wanna hear it." He chuckled.

She blew out a breath. "To put it succinctly, you're hot."

"Everyone is out in this heat," he teased. "I think Juan sweats more than I do. You can probably get some good pictures of him."

103

She punched his upper arm and grinned. "I *know* you know what that means."

"So, you're a stalker, huh?" He laughed.

"Only when it comes to hot guys working on my father's farm."

"Oh, so I'm not the first then?" He feigned offense.

She laughed and mischief twinkled in her eye. "I'll never tell."

"Now I'm going to be self-conscious while I'm working, knowing you might be taking photos of me." He glanced up at the sun. "Speaking of work, it looks like I should be heading back now."

"I'd think that being from an Amish background, you'd be used to random people taking pictures of you."

"You'd think so, huh? But we lived out in the boonies. That sort of thing was more common in the larger communities closer to big towns. I didn't get off the farm all that often."

They began packing up the blanket and fragments of food.

"Thank you for lunch, Azalea."

"Thanks for coming with me."

"I had a good time. You're better company than the guys are."

She laughed. "Well, that's good to know."

He mounted his steed. "So, swimming tomorrow?"

"Yes. But let's save it for after work. I'll take you home."

"You're sure?"

"Yep. Positive. You just remember to bring your swim trunks." She took off in a cloud of dust.

"I will." Joseph happily followed behind.

FOURTEEN

Joseph waded into the lake, the cool water momentarily stealing his breath away. But it was nothing compared to the pounding in his heart the first time he'd seen Azalea in her swimsuit two weeks ago, *and* each time they'd gone to the lake since then. He tried not to notice how wonderful she looked, but it was nearly impossible. He supposed her attire was probably modest compared to the bathing suits he'd seen on some of the mannequins at the store.

However, growing up with mostly brothers and not being involved in youth activities meant his interaction with young women had been minimal. In fact, he'd never seen a woman who hadn't been fully clothed. But Azalea…he'd had to look away and try to keep his focus on other things. Otherwise his mind raced to places it shouldn't go. *God, help me keep my thoughts pure.*

Fortunately, she was covered by the water now. "You coming in?" Her baby blues sparkled, now reflecting the cerulean lake. It was interesting how the lake took on the sky's hues, then in turn, replicated in Azalea's eyes.

"I'm making my way."

"Are you going to come out more than a few feet this time?"

"Uh…we'll see."

She frowned. "You *do* know how to swim, don't you?"

"Let's just say I know how to keep from drowning." He grinned.

"You mean dog paddling. Swimming is a lot less taxing on the body. I'd be happy to teach you."

"Ah, no." He waded in up to his chest. Far enough.

She splashed water in his direction. "What are you afraid of, Jonah? I promise I won't let you be swallowed by a whale."

He splashed water back at her and smirked. "Oh, you won't, huh?"

She shook her head.

"You're a strong woman, but I highly doubt you're a match for a whale."

He watched as she disappeared under the water. Where did she go? The water was too murky to see through and the sun's reflection even made it worse. He turned a circle, squinting, attempting to see under the water.

He suddenly felt water pouring over his head and down his neck and gasped. He turned around, expecting to find Azalea but she'd disappeared back into the water. He moved around trying to feel for her in the water, to no avail.

He then felt something clasp around one of his ankles and tug at him, attempting to knock him off balance. He laughed out loud. "You want to play, huh?" Not that she could hear him underwater.

He held his breath and dipped his head underwater. He reached down to where he thought she might be and finally caught hold of her. He guessed it was her arm. He quickly found her waist and pulled her up out of the water.

"Jonah!" She laughed, struggling to break free of his hold.

"Thought you could get me, huh? I may not be a great swimmer, but I'm quite a bit stronger than you."

She stopped struggling and turned in his arms. Her wet hair sent droplets of water down the sides of her face. She was just as attractive as ever, if not more so. He couldn't even imagine a situation where she wouldn't look beautiful.

His sucked in a ragged breath, realizing her closeness. He searched her eyes and a longing like he'd never known coursed through his entire being. What would it be like to kiss a woman? To press his lips to hers and unleash this desire that kindled so strongly in his soul. He lifted his hand to caress her cheek but suddenly stopped. No, he couldn't touch her. What was he doing? He shouldn't be holding her in his arms like this. That was a husband's privilege, and a husband's privilege only.

He wouldn't do it. He couldn't. *Der Herr* said it was good for a man not to touch a woman, save they be married. And they were not. But someday. Lord willing.

Someday.

It took everything in him to fight off this temptation that had taken ahold of him. He reluctantly released her and took a step back. He didn't miss the disappointment that crossed her features. Had she wanted the same thing?

But no. She wasn't his for the taking. And judging by their stations in life, would never be. *God, give me strength.*

"I should go." He made his way toward the shore, briefly glancing back.

"Jonah." She huffed and thrust her palms upward,

bringing water with them. "What's wrong?"

"Nothing." He shook his head, but didn't look in her direction again. "Everything. I—I've got to go."

"Did I do something wrong?" He heard her making her way out of the lake as well. "Jonah, talk to me."

She came and stood in front of him. Thankfully she'd wrapped a towel around her body.

"I can't do this, Azalea."

"Do what?" She frowned.

"I can't be here. With you. Like this."

"Why not?" Her voice shook. He hoped he wouldn't make her cry.

"No, it's not…" He blew out a pent-up breath. "Azalea, you're too much of a temptation for me."

A half-smile tugged her mouth upward. "Is that why…?"

He lifted a hand to her cheek and gazed into her eyes. "I think I'm falling in love with you."

A full smile now blossomed on her face. "You are?"

He nodded and let his hand drop to a safe place.

"Good."

His brow shot up. "Good?"

"Yeah." She stood on her tiptoes and kissed his cheek. "I'm glad I'm not the only one."

"You mean, you…?" He could hardly believe it. Could Azalea *really* be the one? The thought made his spirit soar.

She nodded. "I've never met anyone like you, Jonah. You're…well…perfect."

He laughed. "I'm definitely not that."

"You are to me. I feel like I could spend every minute with you and not get bored. I want to be part of your life."

He swallowed. "You are."

"I want to be more. I want to spend time with you. I want to know everything about you."

"I feel the same way about you." He gulped.

"Do you think that maybe God orchestrated our meeting? That maybe it might be His will that the two of us be together?"

"I was thinking the same thing."

"You were?" Her brow shot upward.

He nodded. "I want to kiss you so badly."

"What's stopping you?"

"I don't know." He shook his head. "I guess I've always felt that that was a husband's privilege."

"You know what, Jonah Millerton? You are too good to be true." She raised her hand to his cheek and the action warmed his entire being. Did she have any idea how much her touch affected him? "But honestly, I can't see us waiting until we're married to kiss. Not when I want to kiss you right now."

"You do?" His voice rose an octave.

"If I do, are you going to try to stop me?"

He shook his head as his gaze caressed her lips. "I'm not sure I possess that kind of strength."

"Good." She lifted on her tiptoes, wrapped her arms around his neck, and pulled him close.

Joseph didn't resist as her soft lips pressed against his own. He savored every second as he returned her kiss, learning as he went along. He wished it would never end.

She pulled back and her eyes twinkled. "I love you, Jonah Millerton."

⌇

Yep, today had officially been the second-best day of his life! The very best day had been at the shelter, when he'd given his life to Christ. It was peculiar how his best days only occurred after being expelled from his community. Had it been necessary for him to separate from his family in order to receive all God had for him? It sure seemed like it.

Now he felt like dancing in public. Running around the block a hundred times. Doing a million jumping jacks. Even if he did, though, he doubted this feeling of exhilaration would ease up. Azalea loved him! She'd kissed him! His first kiss. Ever.

He was certain he wouldn't get a wink of sleep tonight as he rested his head on his pillow.

The *Englisch* life couldn't get much better than this, could it?

Nah, he doubted it.

He was quite certain that Azalea was *the one* his father had told him would come along. The one who'd steal his heart. The one who would occupy all his thoughts. The one whom he'd desire to spend the rest of his life with. He couldn't imagine feeling the same about any other woman. She owned his heart.

But he couldn't get ahead of himself. Right now, to consider her anything more than just a friend would be presumptuous. And foolish. He was tempted to dream, though. After all, she *had* declared her love.

Nee, he wouldn't count his hay bales until they'd been harvested. No telling when a storm might come along and ruin his entire crop. He'd learned that all too well.

He now prayed for his family as he did every evening, but sent up a special prayer of thanksgiving to God for the blessings He'd bestowed upon him.

Would Azalea someday become his *fraa*? If only it were so!

FIFTEEN

Joseph sat next to Azalea on a blanket under the shade of the trees. His gaze turned from the shining water to the beauty beside him. "Tell me about your life. I want to know everything about you."

"Everything? There's not much to tell. I've lived a pretty boring life."

"Boring?" He highly doubted being the daughter of a wealthy farmer was boring. He laughed. "Well if you think that *your* life has been boring, I can't imagine what you'd think about my life."

"I want to hear your story first."

He grimaced. Maybe he shouldn't have brought himself up. Could he tell her about his former life without giving away too many details?

"Hmm…okay. Um, well, I grew up in Southern Indiana. Lived there pretty much my whole life. Wait a minute. You already know about me."

"Some, but not all of it."

"I don't know if I can ever explain all of it." He laughed, albeit a bit nervously. If she only knew the entire truth of his past. Would she still care for him after finding out what a nuisance his brothers believed him to be? Or would her opinion of him change?

"What was it like growing up in an Amish home?"

"Truthfully? *A lot* of work."

She nodded. "The Amish are known for their strong work ethic. I can see that's true when I watch you work. You put everything you have into it. As a matter of fact, it seems like you put everything you have into all you do."

"I try. God says that whatsoever our hands find to do, that we should do it with all our might—as if we're doing it for the Lord."

"That's one of the things I love about you, Jonah. You're so good. Pure. Honest."

What would she think if she knew the entire truth of his past? The hidden part that he *never* wanted to disclose to anyone. Surely, she'd think differently about him. He shook his head. "No. I fail often."

"I understand. You're not perfect. But you *strive* to be. I appreciate that."

"I'm afraid you lift me up too much. That can only lead to disappointment."

"I can't see you ever disappointing me, Jonah."

And there it was. She believed him to be honest, when in fact, she didn't even know his real name.

"Don't say that. I will. I'm human. I will disappoint you. I will fail. Trust me. I know my own thoughts." He sighed. "I don't want to talk about me anymore."

"Wait." She laid her hand on his forearm, sending his temperature up another notch. How did she do that, anyway? "Don't shut me out. Please."

"Okay. What else do you want to know?"

Her tone gentled. "How old were you when your mother died?

"It was when my little brother was born, so eight."

"Only eight?" Her hand splayed over her chest.

"Yeah. It was most difficult on my dad. And probably my sister too. All the household chores fell on her shoulders after that. It's not easy taking care of ten males."

"Ten?" She screeched.

He could have kicked himself for sharing so much unnecessary information with her.

"Poor girl. How old was she?"

Azalea had no idea of the gravity of Dinah's situation. What would she think if she knew about all his sister had gone through? About his brothers and the evil they'd done? If Azalea's father wasn't against him now, he'd have plenty of reason to be if his true identity were to ever be revealed. That was precisely why she could never, ever know. Besides, he'd promised *Dat* he'd never tell anyone about their family's secret past. And he'd never break his promise to *Dat*. Not even for Azalea.

"She's quite a bit older than me. My father married young. After his first wife passed away, he married my mom."

"So, how many children did your mom have?"

"Just two. My brother and me."

"That's crazy. I can't even imagine growing up in a household that large."

"It was crazy at times, for sure. But Dad tried his best to keep everyone in line."

"So, how did you end up here?"

This was one of the questions he'd been dreading. How could he avoid the true circumstances of his forced departure from the Amish yet not lie to her? *Help me, Lord.*

He shrugged. "God. He allowed me to meet a great man who introduced me to the Bible. He showed me how I could have eternal life and I accepted Christ as my Saviour."

She frowned. "But I thought... Don't the Amish read the Bible?"

"Yeah, some. But our Bible was in German so I never really understood much of it. I had heard about Jesus, but I'd never heard that you can be saved and know you're on your way to Heaven. I'd always thought that I had to live a good Amish life."

"Wow. Why didn't you have an English Bible that you could understand?"

"You know, I'm not really sure. It might have been forbidden."

"Forbidden? A Bible?"

"I don't know. I never asked those kinds of questions. Asking too many questions was usually frowned upon. We were just taught that we did things the way we did because that was what our ancestors did. If it was good enough for them, it was good enough for us."

"Wow."

"Okay. *Your* turn. Tell me about you."

"I told you that my life was boring. And now that I know your background, you'll really think so."

"Nothing about you could be boring to me." He trailed her arm lightly with his finger.

"Okay, tell me what you want to know, Jonah Millerton."

"Have you always lived here?"

"Yes."

119

"How did your father become wealthy?"

"My grandfather passed down a decent-size farm to my father. My father used the increase from the crops and made some wise investments."

"What kind of investments?"

"Mostly stocks. He had a good eye. He bought low and sold high. He invested in some up and coming companies and now he can basically do what he wants."

"So, he manages this property?"

"Not really. He hires it out. My dad isn't really much of a farmer. He actually went to school to become a minister."

"Wait. Your father's a preacher?"

"Yes and no."

"What do you mean?"

"He's sort of an on-call preacher. He doesn't have a congregation of his own."

"Hmm… that's interesting." He scratched his head. "Do you and your dad have a close relationship?"

"I guess so. I was always closer to Mom, but Dad and I have become closer since she died."

He frowned, thinking of his father. He was surely closest to his father than anyone else had been. He briefly wondered if Benjamin had taken his place.

"Tell me about your mother."

"She was my best friend. I could talk to her about anything. I miss her so much sometimes." A tear slid down her cheek followed by another. "I wish I could have just another day with her, you know?"

He knew exactly. What he wouldn't give to see *Dat* again.

"I'm sorry." He pulled a handkerchief from his pocket and handed it to her.

She wiped her eyes, then handed it back.

"No, you keep it."

She stared down at it, as though noticing it for the first time. She fingered the lace corner and delicate embroidery. "This is lovely."

He smiled. "*Jah.*"

"Did you get it from a girl?" Her brow arched. Was she jealous?

"Yeah."

She shook her head and handed it back. "No, thank you. I don't want to take it from you."

"My *schweschder*. It was from my sister. She made me two of them." Fortunately, it was one thing from home he'd had with him the day he met his demise at his brothers' hands. He pushed the hankie back toward her. "Please. Keep it. I want you to have a way to remember me. To remember our friendship."

"Remember you?" She frowned and moved her

thumb over the embroidered flowers. "Where are you going? I didn't realize you planned on leaving the area."

"I'm not sure where we'll go next." He shrugged. "But it seems like everything good in life comes to an end at one point or another." He thought of *Mamm* dying, of his brothers' actions, of losing *Dat* for reasons unknown to him. His heart grieved. Would he ever see *Dat* alive again? It seemed unfair that their living years must be spent apart.

Azalea grew quiet. "I'd hoped this could be a lifelong friendship," she whispered.

"We can hope. As a matter of fact, I'm hoping for more than just friendship. Either way, I still want you to keep that."

The corner of her mouth lifted a little and she folded the handkerchief and tucked it into her pocket. "Thank you, Jonah. I'll cherish it. And as far as I'm concerned, I already consider you much more than just a friend."

She leaned close and kissed his cheek.

"I know." He wanted so badly to hold on to that hope. But for some reason their relationship seemed like a lathering bar of his sister's soap that would slip through his fingers at any moment.

Was God sending him some sort of warning? Preparing him for something he couldn't foresee?

SIXTEEN

Six months later...

"Thank you for volunteering to work inside." Mrs. Brandenburg, the estate's owner, seemed to be an overly cheerful person. To him, it almost seemed fake.

He silently chided himself for judging this woman before he even had a chance to know her. She was a friend of Azalea's family, so she must be a sincere person. His initial assessment was most likely mistaken. Although he was usually a pretty good judge of character. He had his older brothers to thank for that quality.

He wanted to tell this woman that he hadn't actually volunteered, he simply agreed to the boss' request. Wasn't that what an employee was supposed to do?

"What did you need done?"

"Well, I have some ceiling fans that I need to have installed and a couple of the rooms need to be painted." She pinned him with a stare which made him uncomfortable. "Are you capable of completing those tasks?"

"I believe so." He looked away.

"Good. Now that we have that established, I'd like you to join me in the sunroom for some tea."

"Oh...uh...no, thank you. I really should get to work on those things you mentioned. I get paid to work."

"Well, since my husband and I are doing the paying, I insist." She smiled like the Cheshire Cat.

Joseph swallowed. "Ok. You're the boss."

"Follow me." She led the way into a beautiful room furnished with white leather couches and colorful accent pillows. "Do have a seat. I'll be right back."

After she left the room, he moved and stood at the window, looking out at the magnificent view. Trees, barns, homes, and fields dotted the landscape and the location of the owners' home gave an optimal view of all of it.

"Pretty, isn't it?"

He startled at her hand on his shoulder blade and stepped away to the side. "*Jah.*"

"I thought this hill was the perfect place for a home."

He turned from the window and took a seat on the couch farthest from where she stood.

"Tea." She handed him a glass of iced tea, then sat down beside him.

Why did she have to sit right next to him when there was a whole nother empty couch?

"Do you like it?" She traced her bottom lip with her finger, as though she wanted him to notice her mouth.

He swallowed. "Uh…yeah, the tea's *gut*."

"Goot?"

"It's good."

"Oh, I'm glad you like it." Her voice was subtle, sultry. She boldly placed her hand on his thigh and it sent off all kinds of alarms in his head.

He bolted from the couch and placed the glass of tea back onto the tray. "I better get to work."

She stood too and quickly approached him, putting her hands on his chest. "We have time before you begin work." She pressed close.

He stepped back. "No! Your husband…he's trusting me to do a job. Besides, it is wrong. It would displease the Lord."

He practically ran from the room, doing his best to catch his breath. He'd never been around a woman so bold in her intentions. How could she approach him like that when she already had her own husband? The thought baffled him.

Did Azalea have any idea that their family friend behaved herself in such a fashion? Surely, they couldn't know this about her.

If he was going to do this job, he needed to stay as far away from that woman as possible. But how could he since all the work he'd be doing here was inside the home? He'd have to be sure and keep busy and avoid the female owner like strong drink.

"That ceiling fan looks nice."

Oh, no. It was her again. Fortunately, he'd had some reprieve the past few days since she'd been busy with errands. He hoped she'd abandoned her foolish notions of any type of relationship between them.

He turned from his place on the ladder to greet her out of common courtesy. "Thank you."

"When you're finished, I have something else that needs to be done in the room down the hall."

"Okay, it'll be about ten more minutes." He didn't even glance her way this time. The last thing he desired was to encourage her in the least.

"Great. It'll be the one with the door slightly open."

He nodded, not wishing to speak any more words to her and be about the task at hand.

Ten minutes later, he found the room with the door open and stepped inside. He looked around, then heard the door behind him close.

"You made it." The voice was back. The woman stepped behind him and quickly clutched the flannel that he had draped over his shoulder earlier when it had gotten too warm.

He turned around just as she tossed his flannel onto a winged-back chair. His mouth dropped open at the sight of her. She wore a very short dress-thingy made of some kind of see-through material he never would have imagined actually existed. That shouldn't exist, he decided. He found it difficult not to stare, but forced himself to look away.

"It's okay. You may look."

No, he didn't *want* to look! He wanted to scrub the image from his mind and never recall it again. He was too stunned to say anything. Like a possum frozen in the middle of the road while a semi headed straight for it.

He refused to look upon another man's wife. He didn't even have to ask why she was dressed that way. He gulped as his heart galloped almost uncontrollably. What she wanted was as clear as the crystal in the chandelier that hung in the main foyer.

Him.

"You like what you see?" She stepped close and whispered in his ear. "It can all be yours, Jonah." She began unbuttoning his shirt.

He had to get out of there.

He finally found his voice. "No, I can't do this! I won't. It is wrong. God wouldn't be pleased. And your husband…"

He ran from the room without looking back. He determined then and there he would not return to this house. No matter what.

He was already out the door when he heard a piercing scream, but he would not go back in to see what had happened. No, he'd never enter this home again.

SEVENTEEN

"That was a wonderful supper. Thank you." Joseph smiled, leaned down, and kissed the cook as he set his dishes into the sink. It was *wunderbaar* having a woman in his home. He hoped that one day it might be a permanent thing. But that was up to *Der Herr*.

He was pretty certain this was how *Dat* had must've felt about *Mamm* before they married.

Azalea lightly pushed him away and continued rinsing debris off the plate she held. "Nope. None of that. We need to wash up these dishes then *you* need to study. No getting out of it." She pointed a finger at him.

He sighed. "It seems like that's all I do lately. Wasn't getting my driver's license enough? Can't we take a break?"

"Well, if you want to pass the HSE with flying colors, you're going to need to learn this stuff. You can take a break *after* you pass the test." She bumped his hip with her own. "We'll do something special when you're done. I promise."

He liked the sound of that.

"But I'll probably just forget it all as soon as I take the test." It seemed pointless to memorize a bunch of random facts knowing he'd probably just forget them. And never use them. He'd got along this far without knowing these things.

"You'll remember some of it."

He picked up a dish towel and began drying the dishes she set in the rack. "I'm going to remember that part about celebrating."

He covertly studied her as she stood at the sink. She was so smart. And beautiful. And industrious. As a matter of fact, he couldn't find anything about her that he *didn't* like. She'd make a wonderful wife. Just as soon as he felt secure enough that he could provide for her, he planned to approach her father and ask for her hand in marriage. That alone was reason enough to push forward with the HSE. He'd do anything to win her father's approval.

Azalea had wanted to introduce him to her father already, but he wanted to wait until the time was right—when all his ducks were in a row. He didn't want to give the man *any* reason to reject him.

His mind went back to the ordeal at work today. "Azalea? How well does your family know the Brandenburgs?"

"Pretty well. My mother went to high school with Mrs. Brandenburg. They were friends."

He nodded. "Oh."

"We don't see each other too often. And it's been quite a bit less since Mom passed on. We occasionally go to dinner parties and such." She turned from the sink. "Why do you ask?"

He shrugged. He didn't know much about dinner parties, but he knew he'd never want to be in the same room with the seductive Mrs. Brandenburg again.

He'd wanted to tell Azalea about the events of the day, but didn't know how to bring it up. The whole situation had been terribly awkward and embarrassing. Maybe he should just keep it to himself for now. He didn't want Azalea to think less of her mother's friend.

But then again, she probably should know. "Well, when I was wor—"

He heard a knock on the door of his small apartment. He tossed the towel on the counter. "*Ach*, someone's here. I wonder who it could be. Just a minute."

He moved to the entry and pulled the door open, not thinking twice about checking through the peephole. Back home in his Amish community, he couldn't ever remember locking the doors.

"Are you Jonah Millerton?" One of two uniformed police officers asked.

"Yes." He frowned. *What could be wrong?*

In a split second, he spun around involuntarily and his arms were yanked tightly behind his back. Something cold and metal closed hard around his wrists. It brought back memories inside a garbage truck.

"What...?" He couldn't even formulate the words.

Azalea walked into the room at that moment.

"Jonah, what's wrong? What's going on?" Azalea met his eyes with dismay. They probably mirrored his own.

"I don't know!" His breathing became shallow.

"You have the right to remain silent. Anything you say can and will be used against you in a court of law. You have the right to an attorney. If you cannot afford..." The officer continued reading, but all Joseph could hear were the tumultuous thoughts in his head.

"What? I don't... What did I do?" He hated the fact that tears pricked his eyes and he couldn't wipe them away. What must Azalea be thinking?

"Does attempted rape ring a bell, buddy?" The officer handled him roughly, he guessed on purpose.

Rape? The word sounded familiar but he was unsure of what it meant. *Wait a minute, isn't that what had happened to Dinah? Wait, what?* His thoughts began spinning out of control.

"Seems to me that would be an easy thing to remember," the other officer added his two cents. Implying that he'd *already* committed a crime.

But he was innocent! He had done no such thing—*wouldn't* do something like that. Ever.

His breathing became shallow. "What…?" The word was more like a whisper.

No answer.

"Attempted rape?" Azalea chirped. "What do they mean, Jonah?" Her eyes went wild like a spooked horse.

"I-I don't know, Azalea." All he knew was that everything was happening so fast, he could hardly think straight.

The officers led him by his biceps and one of them opened the door to the back of a police car. He looked around while neighbors stared back at him, glaring and shaking their heads. Azalea looked on in sheer horror.

I'm innocent. He wanted to shout the words. To vindicate himself. To let the world know that he'd done absolutely nothing worthy of this harsh treatment. But instead, he remained silent.

"Duck your head."

He did as told, right before he was shoved onto the

hard plastic backseat of the patrol vehicle. The door slammed shut and in less than a minute he was sliding back and forth as the cop mercilessly drove toward the police station.

God, what's happening here? Please be with me. Guide me. Help me.

EIGHTEEN

Sorrow encompassed Joseph's heart as he sat in what the officers had called a 'holding tank.' Was he really being accused of the exact same horrors that had befallen his sister? How could that be? He hadn't even touched the woman. He *wouldn't* touch her.

He'd only sought to please *Der Herr*. Had he failed? What had he done wrong?

Perhaps he had lost favor with *Gott* because he was no longer Amish? No, that couldn't be right. Could it? It was true that he wasn't Amish anymore. But didn't God still watch out for those who weren't part of the Amish church? After all, there were many millions of people in the world. He used to think that God was so exclusive, so unapproachable, that only the Amish were His chosen people. But now he knew better. What about the Jews? Didn't they claim to be God's chosen

135

people? And what about the Catholics? Didn't they claim to be the one true church? Along with who knows how many other religious establishments? These were things he'd never even considered in the past, not before meeting Robert, the man at the Rescue Mission.

This was not the God that he had read about in his Bible. The God he had read about—Jesus—came to seek and to save that which was lost. The God he learned about died for the *whole* world. *For God so loved the world...* The God he knew about was not willing that *any* should perish but that *all* should come to repentance.

Jah, he was quite certain that these narrowly inclusive groups had it wrong. Hadn't Robert read that *Der Herr* wanted *all* men to be saved, not just a select few? Jesus died for every person. It was up to each individual to decide whether they wanted to accept his free gift of eternal life or whether they wanted to try to get into Heaven on their own merits.

God, what am I doing here?

So much for doing great things for God, as Robert had supposed he would. What good could come of being locked in a prison? Not much, that he could imagine.

The only thing he could think of is that he must have somehow failed God. But how? What did he do to deserve this?

Joseph felt like he'd been walking around in a haze for the past week. He still couldn't get the look on Azalea's face out of his mind. Disappointment. Shock. Mortification. So many emotions had surfaced, he couldn't even identify all of them. He had no doubt that she'd now lost all confidence in him. If he'd ever hoped to have a future with her, he could probably forget about it now. Those dreams may as well be buried along with the trash heap he'd crawled out of three and a half years ago.

His prison cell opened and two officers walked in. They slapped a pair of handcuffs on him and fastened his feet in a restraint as well. What was going on?

"Your court date is today. You'll meet with an attorney first, then you'll stand before the judge."

He swallowed. He'd never pictured himself in court. Really had no idea how any of this process worked.

They led him out to a van and helped him inside, then shut the door. The two officers that had escorted him out went back from where they'd come from. Another officer—a different one—sat at the steering wheel and manned the vehicle, while yet another one sat beside him, gun at the ready.

He hated this feeling of being a criminal when he'd

done nothing he knew of that could be considered a crime. What had happened?

When they arrived at an impressive stately building that he guessed was the courthouse, he was immediately ushered into a room with a large desk and a couple of chairs. Joseph was directed to take a seat. One of the officers stayed in the room with him. His eyes roamed the room and he took in its features, doing his best to distract himself from reality. From asking all the questions he had no answers to.

A man in a suit walked in and shook his hand. "My name's Mr. Meyers and I'll be representing you in court today. I'll need you to tell me what happened between you and Mrs. Brandenburg."

Joseph swallowed. "I had been working in her home and she asked me to put up a ceiling fan in one of the rooms. When I went in, she closed the door behind me."

"Was she in the room too?"

"*Jah*. I didn't know she was in there at first. I think she must've been behind the door because I hadn't seen her until I walked in and she closed the door."

"Go on."

"When I turned around, she was wearing a not-so-*gut* dress."

"What do you mean by 'not so good'?"

"I could…uh…see through it." He swallowed, not

wanting to remember the regretful image now permanently stamped in his mind.

"Okay. What happened next?"

"She said something like, 'Do you like what you see? It could be yours.'" He blew out a breath.

Mr. Meyers nodded.

"And then I said that I couldn't do what she was asking. That it would displease the Lord and her husband."

"And then?"

"Then I ran out of the room, out of the house. I told myself that I'd never go back to work there again."

"Anything else you'd like to add?"

He closed his eyes, willing this nightmare to go away. "No. I don't think so."

NINETEEN

*J*oseph briefly lifted his eyes and searched the occupants of the courtroom to see if Azalea had come to his hearing. He wasn't sure whether he'd wanted her to be here or not. Apparently, she hadn't showed up yet. It was probably for the best anyhow.

He didn't even *want* to look at the woman who sat on the seat next to the judge's bench. How could she make up these lies about him? Did she not have a conscience? Did she not care how this made him appear in the eyes of everyone around? His friends? His co-workers? His loved ones? Did she have no regard for how her words defamed his character?

He longed to run out of this courtroom, away from all those who looked upon him as though he'd actually done the terrible thing he was being accused of.

All his life, he'd tried to be an honest, upright man— the person he thought God wanted him to be. No, he wasn't perfect but he sincerely tried to keep a clean slate. As far as he knew, he'd done nothing wrong. Nothing for his brothers to have wanted to kill him. Nothing for this woman to accuse him of.

He wouldn't blame God. No, he trusted Him. But he couldn't help but question why these things were happening to him. How was this going to bring glory to God? What did God have planned?

"Is this your shirt?" Mrs. Brandenburg's lawyer asked Joseph, pulling him out of his reverie.

Joseph frowned. He'd forgotten all about his shirt. "Yes."

His lawyer looked at him and frowned. He whispered in his ear, "You didn't say anything about a shirt."

"I forgot about it," he whispered back and shrugged. When he'd bolted out of the Brandenburgs' home, the last thing on his mind was his forgotten flannel.

"Mrs. Brandenburg. Can you tell us about this shirt?" Her lawyer asked in front of all the people.

"Yes." She looked directly at the judge. "Your honor, I was in my room when Mr. Millerton came in. He looked at me in a very sensual way and said that I was the most beautiful woman he'd ever seen. He removed his shirt and threw it onto my bed. He said that we could lock the door and do something while my husband was away. I refused and told him that I was a married woman. That's when he reached for my blouse and pulled the buttons loose. It ripped when I tried to pull away from him. I began screaming and that's when he ran out of the house." She broke down in tears and buried her face in her arms.

What? That's not what happened at all!

"That's not true!" Joseph stood up and desperately looked to the judge—the jury—anyone who would hear him. But everyone seemed to ignore him.

"That is enough." The judge said to the witness on the stand. "You may take your seat, Mrs. Brandenburg."

"*None* of it is true!" Joseph insisted.

"There will be silence in this courtroom!" The judge pounded the gavel and frowned at Joseph. "You have already given your testimony, Mr. Millerton. Sit down or I will have the bailiff haul you out."

Mr. Meyers reached for Joseph's arm then shook his head. "Don't talk. You're not helping."

Joseph sighed and sat down.

Mrs. Brandenburg's lawyer spoke again. "I'd like to call Miguel Montoya to the stand."

A short Hispanic man now sat in the witness stand next to the judge's bench. Joseph recognized him as one of Mrs. Brandenburg's employees.

"Please state your name and how you know Mrs. Brandenburg."

"I work for Mr. and Mrs. Brandburg for five year." He said in broken English. "I work in garden."

"Will you tell us what you saw on the afternoon of October seventeenth?"

"Yes. I working in garden. Prepare bush for cold. I hear scream. Jonah come running out of house. Then Ms. Brandburg come too. She cry and hold her shirt together."

"And was her shirt torn?"

"Yes. It had tear in middle. She also hold Mr. Jonah's shirt in other hand. Said he try hurt her."

The lawyer held up the blouse in question. "Is this the shirt Mrs. Brandenburg was wearing?"

"It look same, yes."

Her lawyer frowned. "Did Mrs. Brandenburg appear upset?"

"Yes. She cry. She very sad."

"Mr. Montoya, you said you have been working for Mrs. Brandenburg for five years, correct?"

"Si. Jes."

"Has anything like this ever happened in the past? Has, as Mr. Millerton claims, Mrs. Brandenburg ever tried to seduce any other workers? That you know of?"

"No."

The attorney looked pointedly at the jury then to the judge. "I have no further questions, Your Honor."

The judge looked to Joseph's lawyer. "Would you like to cross examine Mr. Montoya?"

"If I may, Your Honor." Mr. Meyers stood up and approached Mr. Montoya. "Mr. Montoya, how long would you say it was between the time Mr. Millerton ran out of the house and the time Mrs. Brandenburg screamed?"

"Not too long. Maybe ten second."

"And how long after the time Mr. Millerton came running out of the house would you say that Mrs. Brandenburg ran out?"

He shrugged. "Maybe one and half, two minute."

"And would you say that was ample time for Mrs. Brandenburg to have changed her clothing?"

"Objection, Your Honor!" Mrs. Brandenburg's lawyer called. "Speculation."

"Your Honor, I'm simply trying to establish that there was indeed ample time for the plaintiff to have changed her clothing." Mr. Meyers reasoned. "It's completely relevant."

"Objection overruled." The judge said, then looked at Mr. Montoya. "You may answer the question."

"I think there may be enough time to change, but I not there." He shrugged with his palms up.

"Thank you. I have no further questions, Your Honor." Mr. Meyers sat back down next to Joseph.

Joseph held his breath. This was not looking good for him. But since he and Mrs. Brandenburg were the only two people present at said event, they were the only ones who knew the truth.

And God, He knew the truth. *Please God, please get me out of this mess,* Joseph silently prayed.

A half hour later, Joseph sat in stunned silence as the judge read the verdict.

"The jury finds the defendant guilty of attempted sexual assault." The judge and jury had believed everything the woman said, even though it was all lies.

He could hardly believe that someone could be so convincing. He'd even almost felt guilty as she sat there and told her sob story. The tears flowed so naturally as though he'd actually done the things she'd accused him of.

He'd known before they'd even read the sentence what it would be. He could tell by the way the jury acted as Mrs. Brandenburg told her story full of deceit.

How could someone just make these things up and send an innocent person to prison? Why would anyone do that? He hadn't done *anything* to her. He'd only refused her advances. He'd stood for what was good and right. Actually tried to protect not only his own reputation but hers as well.

Why, God? Why didn't You fight for me? You know I'm innocent!

And then it hit him.

Hadn't the same thing happened to the Lord? Jesus had been put on trial. Been accused of things He hadn't done. Then He was sentenced—not only to scourging, but to death as well. And what had *He* done when all these things were taking place? He hadn't defended Himself. He'd remained silent. His closest friends abandoned him—betrayed Him, even. And when the worst of His fears came true, He not only willing gave up His life—He also forgave those who caused His death.

Shame descended on Joseph like the storm clouds now gathering outside. His predicament wasn't anywhere near as dire as the Saviour's had been. He bowed his head in humility. *Lord, I'm sorry. Please forgive me of my faults and help me to be more like You. Help me to keep my eyes fixed on and to trust You.*

He knew it'd be nearly impossible to do. But he would try. And when he was accused, he hoped that he could keep silent as the Lord had. He didn't need to defend himself. God knew the truth.

Joseph couldn't help but admit that he'd felt somewhat forsaken, though, as the van traveled back to the prison. What was God's plan in all this? And why hadn't God spared him the humiliation? He did his best to trust, but he couldn't help but ask these questions.

My grace is sufficient for thee. And just like that, the verse came to him. As though God Himself were right there with him. And He was, Joseph realized.

I know, Lord. I'm trying.

His sentence had been a minimum of two years. Not terribly long, but still unjust considering it was for a crime he hadn't committed.

How much would his life change in two years? How much would Azalea change? Would *Dat* still be alive even? Was he alive now? Was he praying for him now? Joseph sure hoped so. Because he needed prayer now more than ever.

Please strengthen my faith, Lord.

TWENTY

*J*oseph wiped his sweaty palms on his orange prison pants, courtesy of the Indiana State of Corrections. He was looking forward to this visit, and not looking forward to it at the same time. He wondered if adding Azalea to his list of approved visitors would prove to be a mistake. How would their visit go?

She hadn't been in the courtroom when he'd been arraigned. He didn't know why but he guessed that somehow her father must've found out and most likely forbid her to go. It was probably for the best anyway. He hadn't wanted Azalea to hear about the things he'd been accused of. Although he was certain that she had probably found out by now.

But Azalea knew him. She knew he wouldn't do something like what he'd been accused of. Didn't she?

He now stared at her through the thick glass barrier as she sat down across from him. She was so beautiful.

149

How did God ever see fit to let the two of them find one another? Perhaps it had been too good to be true.

Azalea seemed fidgety now. She put her arms on the small countertop in front of her then put them down at her sides. Was she scared to be here? It was most likely her first time behind the walls of a correctional facility.

She wouldn't look him in the eye.

"So, is it true?" Her voice trembled as she spoke the barely-audible words.

No 'hello.' No 'how are you doing?'

Joseph stared at Azalea and noticed the tears in her eyes. *She* thought he was guilty too? If there was anyone whom he'd thought he could count on, anyone who wouldn't just assume, surely it was her. A knife cut through his chest. Because if *she* didn't believe in his innocence, no one would.

"What do *you* think?" He couldn't hold his sharp tone. Couldn't she at least give him the benefit of the doubt?

"I…I don't know." A tear escaped her eyelashes and traveled down her cheek. "I don't *want* to believe it."

"But you do." He said flatly. "You're just like everybody else. I thought you knew me, Azalea." Disillusionment ripped through his heart. Why had he expected her to be any different?

"I thought I did too…"

"You know what? Believe whatever you want. That's what matters, right? Who cares what the truth is. I'm in prison so I *must* be guilty."

"What do you want me to say, Jonah? You've been *convicted* of attempted rape. The judge and jury heard the testimonies and considered the evidence. A conviction usually means that a person *is* guilty of what they've been accused of. How am I supposed to deal with that? What do you expect me to believe? That the charges, the evidence, the testimonies are all false?"

He shrugged. He was so disappointed in her he couldn't even find the words to say.

"I can't believe…and with Mrs. Brandenburg?" She shook her head as a tear trailed her cheek. "Why were you alone with her in the first place? What were you doing in her *bedroom*? And you were obviously there."

"I was *working*, Azalea! But what does it matter anyway? She's the one with the money and she's sought to destroy my life." He scoffed. "All anyone needs in this world is a little bit of money, right? You can get the judge to give whatever verdict you wish because you throw some money at him." He shook his head. "You're rich. *You* should know…"

"That's not true."

He ignored her words. "But what do I know? I'm just the poor, uneducated idiot." He turned away.

"No, you're not."

The sooner they parted ways, the better for both their sakes. Even if she *did* believe he was innocent, which she didn't, who knows what else Mrs. Brandenburg might come up with and how many years he'd be in prison? And what good would he be to Azalea then? It's not like her father would ever approve of their relationship now anyway. "I'm surprised your father let you come here."

"He didn't. He doesn't know I'm here. He wants me to stay away from you."

"Then why are you here?" He couldn't help his sharp tone.

He heard her gasp. "I thought… You know what, Jonah? I have *no* idea. Goodbye!" She stood and wiped her eyes, shaking her head in the process.

"Don't come back."

She began walking away, then stopped and spun around. He saw the tears, which were now many, flowing from her eyes. "Oh, you don't have to worry about that. I won't. Ever." She took off at a brisk pace, wiping her cheeks as she went.

Joseph dropped his head in his hands the moment she was out of sight, emotion filling him. *God, I didn't want it to end that way. I'm sorry. I failed You once again.*

152

Why is this happening? I feel so helpless. These circumstances are beyond my control. I'm frustrated that I can't do or say anything to defend myself. Why am I here, God?

TWENTY-ONE

"Time for your classification." A correctional officer said as he escorted Joseph down a hall toward an administration office.

"What do you mean?"

The officer chuckled. "Did you think you were going to stay behind steel bars in a brick cell the entire time you're here?"

Joseph shrugged. He had no idea *what* to expect. He'd always *thought* that prison meant behind bars.

"They'll tell you which unit you're in. If you don't mess up, chances are you'll stay there until your release."

"What's a unit?"

"It's like a large dormitory. Several bunk rooms line the walls. A big open recreation space in the middle where the TV is."

"A TV? In prison?"

"You really don't know anything, do you?"

"Not about prison." Did everyone know what prison was like? Surely he hadn't been the only one unaware. He couldn't imagine Azalea knowing these things. But maybe she did? It wasn't really something that had come up in conversation on their dates.

"Well, you'll be getting a crash course then. Haven't you ever watched any prison movies?"

"No."

"Not even *Escape from Alcatraz*?"

"Never heard of it."

"You've never heard of Alcatraz? Not that *that* movie would help you out any. Things were quite a bit different back then. You been living under a rock or something?"

"No. Just never watched much TV."

"Ah, that explains it. Well, you're probably better off anyway." The officer shrugged. "A word of advice—when you go to take your showers and such, don't talk to anyone else, don't look at anyone else. Mind your own business and get out of there ASAP."

"Okay." Joseph frowned and forced out a breath.

The officer pulled the door open and motioned him inside. "Well, here we are. Good luck."

"Mail call!" One of the correctional officers called out as he walked through the inmates' living area.

Joseph didn't bother to turn around. Since he had no contact with his family and his friends and coworkers seemed to have forgotten about him, he never expected to receive mail.

The officer stopped at the entryway to his bunk room. "Jonah Millerton?"

Joseph's head shot up. *I have mail?* Who could have written to him?

"Yeah. That's me."

The man handed him a plain white envelope. He examined the handwriting. It appeared to be feminine. He wasn't completely sure, but he guessed it was from Azalea.

Had she changed her mind about him? Had God softened her heart? Was she seeking to correspond with him while he was in prison? A thrill of hope zinged up his spine. *Lord, please let it be so*.

Without another thought, he tore the letter open. His eyes devoured every word.

Dear Jonah,
   I hardly know what to write.
   How could you?
   I spoke with Miranda Brandenburg. I can't believe it.

I trusted you! I gave you my heart. I can't believe I fell for your lies.

I can't believe our entire relationship was just an act. You put on a better performance than any Hollywood actor, that's for sure.

I don't know what to say to you. I am so angry. And hurt. I just want to scream at you for charging into my life and stealing my happiness! For making me believe you're someone that you aren't! You held my heart in your hands and you've taken it and ripped it to pieces!!!

I don't know why I'm even telling you this. You probably get some sick sense of satisfaction from other people's suffering. Well, before you laugh, you can just rest assured that God will judge you! That is my comfort.

Just stay away from me. If you get out of there, don't come looking for me because I won't give you the time of day. I don't want to have anything to do with you. I've already wasted too many precious hours on you.

I hope I never have to see you again.
Goodbye forever!
Azalea

He let the letter slip through his fingers and glide gracefully to the floor, ignoring the sharp sting of the papercut that sliced through his finger in the process. It didn't matter. Nothing mattered. He'd lost Azalea. For good. Forever.

The words on the page assaulted his heart as though each one were a sword piercing through his flesh. He realized in that moment that he really hadn't known Azalea at all. The Azalea he knew would believe the best in him. The Azalea he knew wouldn't write these harsh words. The Azalea he knew was loving and kind. The Azalea he knew would encourage him to have faith, that God was in control. The Azalea he knew would tell him that she still loved him and that she'd be waiting for the day they could marry.

He was *so* sure that she was the one—that she'd been sent straight from God! Showed how much he knew.

He dropped to his knees and leaned onto his bed, hands folded in front of his face, not caring if anyone walked in. *God, I don't know if I can do this. I don't possess the strength. I'm trying, really trying, to hold on to my faith. But it's so so hard. God, I don't want to turn my back on You, but I'm angry right now. What are You doing here, Lord? Is my suffering bringing You glory? Help me. Please see me through this.*

TWENTY-TWO

*J*oseph straightened his bedding once again, convinced he'd die of boredom if he stayed in this place too long. Sure, he'd been to several appointments in as many days. Medical and dental exams, mental health questionnaires, and educational assessments had kept him somewhat busy in the first few weeks, but now he'd settled into the same boring routine.

He was literally counting down the days before he could leave, sometimes even the hours. He never realized how wonderful freedom had been. Being able to get in his vehicle and drive somewhere—anywhere—thanks to Azalea's skillful instruction. Riding horses to the lake on her property, or even just enjoying a quiet night alone in his apartment, had been paradise compared to his current circumstances.

Inmate census counts several times a day—along

with random strip searches, three square bland meals, and activities kept his mind occupied most of the time. He never enjoyed watching television in the common area because most of the shows were indecent. Keeping his morals and pleasing the Lord in a place like this was difficult at best.

Casper, his bunkmate, or 'celly' as the inmates called it, was pleasant but Joseph hoped they'd be able to form a friendship of sorts. He'd met a couple of other inmates who seemed nice enough, but he'd also run into others who seemed to be mad at the world. He did his best to avoid the latter.

Even though he'd been surrounded by men, a grave sense of loneliness had settled in his soul. He didn't know how these men survived without knowing God, because he surely never would. God had been his only hope, his only thread of sanity at times. He would never ever take freedom for granted again.

What he loathed most about this place was the lack of privacy. He couldn't do anything without someone watching him, not even shower or use the restroom. Now he understood what the officer had attempted to convey to him upon his initiation. It was as though personal dignity ceased to exist the moment he walked into the correctional facility.

If only he'd had something decent to read. He'd

perused the limited books in the prison's library but nothing had caught his eye. Casper offered access to the few books and magazines he owned, but they were not for Joseph. Not even a few pages into the book and he'd already encountered more profanity than he'd heard in his entire life. Well, prior to landing in this facility anyway. And he didn't dare peek at his cellmate's uncouth magazines. If the cover was any indication of what was inside, he wanted no part of it. He'd been shocked to learn that such perversion even existed.

Once again, he'd wondered why God had him in a place like this. He couldn't see any benefit whatsoever. Was it a trial of some sort? It was certainly a test of his character—that he knew for a fact.

He realized even more now that he'd definitely been blessed with a wonderful heritage. Growing up in a sheltered Amish community might have seemed strange to some *Englisch* folks, but if this type of garbage was what he was 'missing out' on, he'd take his Amish upbringing any day. He didn't even want to imagine what life had been like for some of these men prior to coming here. Perhaps he'd join another Plain community when he was released.

He felt sorry for his fellow inmates. Most of them had no idea what it was like to walk barefoot through a freshly-plowed field. They had no idea what one of Dinah's delicious meals tasted like. They had no idea what it was like to tend the animals side-by-side with a loving father. They had no idea what a caring community looked like—could probably never even dream of one. *Jah,* he'd been blessed for sure.

There was no doubt he'd be a changed man when he left this wretched place. He just hoped it was for the better. Because, by the look of it, many of these men seemed like they were only changing for the worse.

Desperation thrust him to the ground again. Perhaps another round of push-ups would help dissolve these depressing thoughts and ease his boredom. After that, he'd do sit-ups. Then jumping jacks. Like he'd done day after lonely day. One thing was for sure and certain. If he accomplished nothing else while in prison, he'd at least leave in great physical shape.

How many more hours would it be before his next tasteless meal?

"Would you like to talk?" A man approached Joseph's cell with a correctional officer at his side. He'd spotted the man earlier speaking with some of the other guys.

He pointed to the shirt he wore. "I'm the chaplain."

Joseph frowned, not understanding what the man meant. He then noticed the cross on his shirt's emblem and a book in his hand that he guessed might be a Bible. "A preacher?"

"Yeah, sort of."

"Yeah, I want to talk." Anything would be preferable to this monotonous existence.

The chaplain nodded and the officer opened Joseph's cell and let him in. "Let's sit." The door clinked shut.

"Okay." Joseph blew out a breath and sat on his bed next to the chaplain.

"My name's Hal." He offered his hand and Joseph shook it firmly.

"I'm Jonah." He read kindness in the man's eyes.

Something about him reminded him of his father. Oh, how he missed him now! Surely *Dat* would have believed his innocence. He knew that for a fact. What he wouldn't give to talk to *Dat* right now.

"Do you mind if I pray first, Jonah?"

"That's fine."

The man clasped his hands together and bowed his head. Joseph followed suit.

"Dear beloved Father in Heaven, we thank Thee for another day of life. We ask that You bless our time of fellowship today. May Jonah know the depth of Your love for him. May we both live a life that's pleasing in Your sight. In the name of the Father, the Son, and the Holy Ghost. Amen."

"What would you like to discuss?" Hal asked.

Joseph shrugged. "I don't know, really. I'm just trying to figure out what's going on in my life right now. Why God has me here."

"Do you know God?"

"Yeah. I received Christ as my Saviour about three years ago."

The chaplain smiled and briefly squeezed Joseph's shoulder. "That's great to hear."

Joseph shook his head. "I don't understand. I keep praying to God, but it seems like He isn't hearing my prayers."

"If you're His child, rest assured that He hears your prayers."

"Why is He silent?"

"As long as we are reading God's Word, He is never silent. Is it possible that you don't like the answers He's giving you?"

"That's the thing. I can't read His Word. I don't have a Bible here."

"Oh. Well that's easy to remedy. I'll be sure you get one before I leave today. I always keep extras in the chapel."

Joseph frowned. "I wasn't aware they were allowed in here."

"They're not only allowed, they're preferred. Nothing can change a man's wicked heart like the Word of God. Christian prison ministries have one of the greatest success rates. Government mandated programs can make one change from the outside, but true heart transformation comes from Christ. And when a prisoner sincerely trusts Christ, it is love that compels him to walk in righteousness. He doesn't have to be forced. He's seen where following his own ways lead him."

"You have a point."

"I'll make sure you get your hands on a Bible, Jonah."

"Thank you, Hal. I appreciate that. I'm sure it will be a great help. When you're locked up in here, you need all the help you can get. Trust me."

"Oh, I believe you." He adjusted his glasses. "What are you in here for, if you don't mind my asking?"

Joseph remained silent. He didn't even want to utter the word. "Attempted sexual assault was what they called it."

Hal nodded. "Attempted?"

"Yeah." But he'd rather not talk about that right now. He sighed. "I was accused of something I didn't even do."

Hal was quiet, but seemed to be listening.

"Not only did I not do what I've been accused of, I stood up for what's right. I don't understand why I'm here." Joseph sighed.

"Jonah, we live in a fallen world. This world is under a curse—the curse of sin. The devil is the god of this world. And as long as it is this way, righteousness will not always be rewarded. We know that someday Christ will return and make things right, but until then injustice will reign."

"I wish Jesus would return today."

The chaplain smiled. "Me too. But until He does, we need to realize that our reward is in Heaven. This life is temporary. It will pass quickly. We need to count our sufferings for Christ as joy—as a privilege."

"That's so hard for me right now. Sometimes I feel like it would be better if God just ended my life."

"Jonah, you need to trust Him. He knows what is best—way more than you or I do. God is not unrighteous. He will not forget your labor of love. It's during these hard times that we need Him most. Don't give up on Him, because He'll never give up on you."

"I'm trying. I really am. I know that God must have me in here for a reason. I just can't figure it out." He blew out a breath. "Whatever it is, I hope it's worth it because I lost my girlfriend over it."

"That's a difficult thing, Jonah." Hal rubbed his eyebrow. "We don't always know why God puts us places. But we know that we can trust Him."

"Yeah, I will try." Surely this man was sent from the Lord. "Thank you for coming today, Hal."

"I'm here once a week to speak with the inmates, and another minister and I take turns conducting the chapel services on Sunday afternoons. I'd love to see you there, Jonah."

"I'd love to go. Thank you for inviting me."

The chaplain smiled. "My pleasure."

"Do many of the inmates attend?"

"More than one would expect. I'm guessing quite a few come just to get out for a while. But I think God has them there for a reason—to hear the wonderful Gospel." He winked.

Joseph nodded. "I'm sure you're right."

"Won't you join me in praying for them throughout the week? You never know when God will do a mighty work in their hearts."

"Yes, I'll pray." He didn't have much else to do.

"Thank you, Jonah. I'll be sure to keep you in prayer too."

"I appreciate that."

Thank you, Lord, for showing me that You care and for bringing people like Chaplain Hal into my life.

TWENTY-THREE

*J*oseph closed his eyes as he lay on his bunk and stared at the ceiling. It seemed nearly impossible to get away from all the commotion in this place. Day in and day out it was nothing but noise. It was enough to drive a person insane if they let it. As soon as he made enough money, which would take quite some time with the meager wages he earned working as an orderly here, he'd purchase a pair of headphones and a radio. He took a cleansing breath and tried to drown out the racket with his thoughts.

What was Azalea doing right now? Was she out riding her horse? Was she swimming in the lake? Shopping at the mall with her friends? Did she have any idea how much he missed her? If only she were here to talk to. If only he could gaze into her eyes or hear her laugh. If only he could hold her in his arms just one more time. Who was he kidding? One more time would never do. He wanted to hold her in his arms for the rest of his life.

A pad of paper sitting on the desk caught his eye. If he wrote her a letter, would she respond? Probably not. She'd said she didn't want to see him again, maybe he should just respect that and ignore this desire burning inside.

But why not write to her? The worst that could happen would be that she'd ignore it and throw it in the trash, right? He had nothing to lose.

He forced out breath and practically jumped from the bed. He opened up the notebook and the pencil hovered above it for just a moment before he began to pen the words in his heart.

Dear Azalea,

I'd like to apologize for the words I spoke to you the last time we saw each other. I realize that I can't take them back or make you forget them. Please forgive me.

I received your letter… I'm sorry you feel that way, but I'm afraid there's not much I can do to change your feelings. You must know that I really do care for you whether you believe it or not.

I hope you are well. Have you been riding your horse lately? Swimming in the lake? I miss the times we used to spend together. I'd give anything to be there with you right now. I don't know if I ever thanked you for helping me get my driver's license, so I want to say thank you now.

Thanks for helping me study for the HSE too. I plan to finish my instruction while I'm in here and hopefully take the test. They have classes that I can take every week, but it's difficult for me to study because there's so much noise here.

You'll never know how much I wish I weren't here. If only I could go back and do things differently. I wish I'd never even taken that job at the Brandenburg's. If I would have known what would have transpired, I wouldn't have stepped foot inside that home. But I guess none of us can go back and change our past, can we?

Well, I don't really know what to write. It's...tough here. Really tough. I don't want to bore you with all the details of prison life, so I guess I'll let you go. Freedom is a wonderful gift. Enjoy it.

Please pray for me, if you will.

I think of you constantly.

Sincerely,

Jonah

❧

Joseph carried his tray of food to one of the tables in the cafeteria. "Mind if I sit here with you?"

The man shrugged, not really paying any mind to Joseph.

"I'm Jonah." He offered his hand.

The man grunted and continued eating his food.

Joseph bowed his head and prayed silently. When he lifted it, the men at the table around him were staring. He grabbed his spoon and began eating.

"Jonah, you said?" A robust man sat his utensil down.

"Yeah."

The man dipped his head. "I'm Maverick. Grumpy over here is Alex."

"It's good to meet both of you."

"I Ricardo." Another prisoner said with a thick Hispanic accent.

Joseph smiled. Growing up on an Amish farm didn't expose him to many different cultures. There seemed to be men of several races here in prison. "Nice to meet you too, Ricardo."

"You pray?" Ricardo asked.

"Yes. Do you?"

"Si. Soy católico."

Joseph frowned.

Alex chuckled at Joseph's clueless expression. "He said he's Catholic. Ricardo's English isn't that great. He's got a pretty good understanding though."

"So, what do you guys usually do around here?" Joseph took a bite of his food and again longed for home. What he wouldn't give for one of Dinah's home-cooked meals right now.

"Not much, other than our jobs and classes. Once in a while, there's a game of poker going on in the rec hall. I wouldn't join unless you're good at gambling. Other than that, you're pretty much looking at it." Maverick volunteered. "If I were you, I'd stay away from Max and Wolf."

Joseph frowned. He'd never gambled in his life and he wasn't about to start now. "Max and Wolf?"

"They're at the table behind us. But *don't* look at them. They'll take it as a challenge. Avoid them at all cost."

Joseph leaned forward and whispered. "What do they look like?"

"Wolf's the one with the wolf tattoo on his neck. Max has two silver front teeth and he's about a foot taller than anyone else."

Joseph made a mental note to steer clear of the two notorious prisoners.

"What are you in here for?" Alex asked.

"I'd rather not say." Joseph blew out a breath. "You?"

"Manslaughter," Maverick volunteered.

A chill climbed up Joseph's spine. *Maverick killed somebody?* He immediately thought of his older brothers.

"Everyone will know sooner or later." Alex shrugged. "Possession with the intent to sell."

"Drugs?"

"No. Cats." Alex chuckled. "Yes, drugs."

"Thefts," Ricardo added. "I steal truck."

"Your turn," Alex challenged.

"Attempted sexual assault." Joseph frowned. How he loathed saying those words.

"Oh, man. Don't let Max and Wolf know that. You'll never get a moment's peace."

"I didn't want *anyone* to know." He was dying to add 'because it's not true.' But what was the point? It wasn't like these men had the power to set him free. And if the one he loved most didn't even believe in his innocence…

He sighed. He refused to go down that thought path again.

God, please be with me while I'm here. Protect me from whatever evil is lurking. Help me find favor.

TWENTY-FOUR

*J*oseph sat at a desk across from one of the facility's employees. He waited patiently for the man to render his assessment of the past few months.

"Well, Jonah. I've got good news for you." His tone didn't reflect the enthusiasm his words hinted at.

"What's that?" He kept his cool.

"You've done very well here so far. I'm putting you in charge of mail call."

"Mail call? Really? But I thought that was a job for employees." He rubbed his stubbled chin. He'd need to shave soon.

"We've been short staffed lately, so I was asked to find someone I would trust with the task. That's you. You've been here a year out of a two-year sentence. It looks like you might be eligible for early parole in about six months, *if* you keep up your behavior. Which, something tells me you're a very smart man and you

177

wouldn't do anything to mess that up."

"Not if I can help it." Joseph smiled. "Thanks. Your trust and confidence means a lot to me."

"If anyone can do this job well, you can." He offered his hand. "By the way, congratulations on passing your HSE. You got one of the highest scores I've ever seen come out of this place."

"Oh, wow. Really?" He knew he had Azalea to thank for a lot of that. But he could never do that now. Maybe he should write her another letter. He'd been disappointed that she'd never responded to the one he'd sent—not that he'd expected her to. But way down deep in his heart of hearts, he'd clung to a hope that she might.

"Yep. What do you plan to do when you get out of here?"

"I'll need to find a job. A place to live." He shrugged.

"We can help with that."

His brow jumped. "You can?"

"Yep. It's not much, but it's enough to help you get on your feet."

"That's great. I wondered where I was going to sleep. I could find a Rescue Mission. I'm hoping to contact my old employer, but I'm not sure if he'll want me anymore."

"Well, I'm glad you have a plan, Jonah."

❧

Alex threw the basketball to Joseph, who tossed it to Maverick. Maverick went for a shot, but it bounced off the backboard and flew out of bounds. Joseph ran to retrieve the ball.

Wolf picked up the ball and his eyes ran wild. "Ah, the prison pet! Come and fetch this ball from me and I'll make you my pet, pretty boy."

Maverick, Ricardo, and Alex raced to his side. "Give the boy the ball, Wolf!" Maverick demanded.

It seemed like ever since Casper's bunk was vacated and Maverick moved in, he'd acted as Joseph's protector. He'd been reminded of a verse he'd read in Psalms, *The angel of the LORD encampeth round about them that fear him, and delivereth them.* God had certainly been looking out for him since he'd been here.

"Or, what?" Wolf sneered.

"You don't want to find out." Alex cracked his knuckles.

A correctional officer blew a whistle and quickly assessed the situation. "What's going on here?"

"Nothing." Maverick said. "Wolf's just returning our ball is all."

The officer eyed Wolf. "Is that right?"

Wolf grunted and tossed the ball to Alex. He stomped off.

"I don't want any trouble." The officer glared at each of them.

"Neither do we. Thanks for intervening, Randy." Joseph nodded his appreciation. The last thing Joseph needed was a problem to arise that would jeopardize his parole date.

Thank You, Lord, for Your hand of protection.

"Hey, have any of you been out in the garden lately?" Sometimes Alex came up with the strangest turns of conversation.

"No," they replied in unison.

"Something's going on there. I can't figure out what it is."

"What do you mean?" Joseph asked.

"The plants. They're all dying."

Joseph frowned. "You'll have to show them to me tomorrow."

"I fear they might be dead tomorrow."

"I'll see if I can take a look at them this evening, then. Here." He tossed the ball to Maverick. "I'll be back."

"Where's he going?" Ricardo asked.

"To look at the garden." Joseph heard Alex's reply before he reached the middle of the yard.

He approached the officer. "Do you think I can take a quick look at the garden right now?"

The officer frowned. "What for?"

"Alex says the plants are dying. I want to see what's wrong with them. I might know how to treat them, but it might be too late if we wait till tomorrow."

Another correctional officer approached. "What's going on?"

"He wants to look at the plants." The first officer looked amused.

"Call someone out to escort him to the garden. I have no doubt Jonah means what he says. He's not about to put his parole at risk." He turned to him. "Are you?"

"No way. I just want to see if I can help the plants."

The officer pulled out a radio and a short time later, Joseph was examining the ailing plants. Exactly what he thought.

"We can go back. It's too late to save them." Joseph couldn't help the disappointment in his tone. He knew the garden was a labor of love for Alex.

The officer escorted him back to the yard, and he walked toward the basketball court.

"That was quick." Maverick's ball sailed through the air and swished through the net. "Oh, yeah! Did you see that?"

Ricardo high-fived him.

Joseph sought out Alex on the side of the court. "How long have they been languishing?"

"A week?" Alex shrugged. "I sprayed them, but it didn't help."

"It's too late to save them. I'm sorry."

"Ah, really?" He shook his head. "That's what I was afraid of."

"If I would have known about the plants a few days ago, we might have been able to bring them back. I'm afraid the spray you used probably made matters worse." Joseph frowned.

"What's wrong with them?"

"I'm almost positive it's a parasite. I've seen it before."

"What did you do?"

"I concocted a homemade spray one time and it worked like a charm." He grinned.

"Really? Maybe you should consider patenting it." Alex slapped his back.

"I don't know about that."

"No, I'm serious, man. You could make a killing. Literally." He laughed.

The basketball came flying in their direction and Joseph snatched it in mid-air. "Let's play before our time is up?"

"You bet!" Alex caught Joseph's pass and went in for a lay-up.

TWENTY-FIVE

"**H**ey, Maverick!" Joseph called from his bunk. His friend tossed and turned in his sleep, but it was obvious he was in some kind of turmoil.

"Maverick, wake up!" Joseph moved to his friend's bed and shook his shoulder.

Maverick bolted upright, his breathing labored. He continued to breathe heavily and his eyes locked with Joseph's.

"You okay, man?"

"Yeah, I'm fine." He breathed out slowly. "I had a dream—no, it was a nightmare."

Joseph nodded, letting him know he was available to listen if he wanted to share.

"You sure you want to hear it?"

"Only if you want to share it with me."

"Okay, at first I was reading some kind of letter.

183

Then I was walking down this long hallway. Really, really long. There were two officers—one on each side—walking with me. I was handcuffed. I felt this sense of urgency but I don't know what it meant. I was scared. So scared…"

Joseph's eyes widened and his chin fell. *No, that can't be right. Lord?*

"What? You know what it meant, don't you?"

Joseph stared at him. He didn't want to lie. He also didn't want to tell Maverick what he knew in his heart to be true of his dream.

"Tell me, Jonah. I want to know."

Joseph shook his head and his eyes watered. "No, you don't want to know. It's probably better if you don't. It's bad, man."

"If it's as bad as your expression says it is, I *have* to know." He lightly touched Joseph's shoulder. "I won't be mad at you. I promise."

"Oh, Maverick. I—"

"Just tell me. Please."

Joseph took a deep breath. "You will receive a message regarding your case. It has been determined that you will receive the death penalty. Soon."

Maverick's eyes locked with his. "The…the death penalty?" He swallowed.

"I'm sorry, Maverick."

184

"You don't need to be."

"Look. Maybe I'm wrong. Maybe I just thought it was God showing me and it was really just my imagination."

"No, you're not. I've watched you, Jonah. I've seen this connection you have with the Man upstairs."

Joseph's lips twisted. *Man upstairs?* "Are you referring to God?"

He nodded.

"You can have a connection with God too, Maverick."

"No, I'm beyond God's help. I've done too many bad things."

"You can be forgiven."

"No, I can't. How can God forgive me when I can't even forgive myself? Jonah, you have no idea of all the terrible things I've done."

"It doesn't matter. Not to God."

"Yeah." He scoffed. "That's why I'm getting the death penalty, right?"

Joseph didn't want to push it. Maverick obviously wasn't ready. "If you ever want to talk, let me know. Okay?"

Maverick nodded and stared expressionless at the wall. Tears filled his eyes. No doubt, he'd been contemplating his fate that was sure to come.

God, please help Maverick. Please open a door for me to share Your love with him.

TWENTY-SIX

A blood-curdling scream awakened Joseph from a dead sleep. His heart raced as he tried to gather his bearings. *Jah, I'm in prison. Still. For a crime I didn't commit.*

God, why am I here?

He turned to see Maverick pacing near his bunk.

"Maverick, was that you that hollered?"

He kept walking backing forth, shaking his head, hands trembling, uttering something undecipherable, as though he were in a trance.

"Maverick!"

His prison mate finally realized he was talking to him and snapped out of it. "Huh?"

"You okay?"

"Bad dream." He shook his head. "Bad dream, man." He sat on his bunk and dropped his head into his hands.

Was he crying?

"Wanna talk about it?"

"I…I don't know. It was scary."

Scary? As far as Joseph knew, Maverick wasn't afraid of anything.

"Tell me."

He shook his head. "I already know what it means."

"And?"

"I'm going to hell. I know it. I'm going to hell. The flames. They were all around me. I felt the heat before it even touched me. Then…"

"Then what?"

"I dropped down into this lake. But it wasn't water. It was fire. I was burning. Burning. But I didn't burn up. I just felt the pain. The regret. The torture. I tried and tried to swim out, to climb out, to claw my way out. I couldn't escape." His breathing became shallow. "It was worse than anything I can even imagine."

"*Jah*, that sounds like hell."

"I know I'm going there. I know it." He wrung his hands, shaking his head.

"Maverick." Joseph moved to sit next to his cellmate. "You don't have to. You may not be on this earth much longer, but right now you're *still* alive. We will all die eventually. There's nothing we can do about that. And it's true. You are headed to hell, but you *can* change your fate. You have a choice. God is giving you a chance to escape that. He loves you, Maverick. He doesn't want you to go there."

He finally stopped fidgeting and stared at Joseph as though he had just heard him for the first time. "He doesn't?"

"No. God is not willing that any should perish but that all should come to repentance. Just repent, Maverick. Ask God to save you and wash away your sins. Put your faith and your hope and your trust in Jesus Christ and He will save you."

"How do I know? How can you know?"

"Because His Word says so and God doesn't lie." He stared at the petrified man next to him in the dimness of their cell.

"You're sure?"

"Let me read you a few verses, okay?"

He nodded.

Joseph prayed inwardly that *Der Herr* would get ahold of this man's heart. That He would change him from the inside out and give him new life. Abundant life. Eternal life.

He reached for the Bible next to his pillow and opened it up to verses he'd underlined. He'd read the verses so many times himself that he could probably quote each one by heart, but he wanted to read the actual words to Maverick, not just speak them to him.

"I'm reading in the book of John, chapter three, beginning at verse sixteen."

Maverick shrugged. "It's all Greek to me."

"Okay, I guess I won't give you the references then." He began, speaking the words slowly. *"For God so loved the world, that he gave his only begotten Son, that whosoever believeth in him shall not perish, but have everlasting life. For God sent not his Son into the world to condemn the world; but that the world through him might be saved. He that believeth on him is not condemned: but he that believeth not is condemned already, because he hath not believed in the name of the only begotten Son of God."*

Maverick nodded as though he were taking it all in.

"You know who *Gott's* Son is, *jah?*"

"Um…Jesus?"

"That's right. Jesus was innocent, but He died on the cross like a criminal, and He rose again after three days." He confirmed. "Jesus said, '*I am the way, the truth, and the life. No man cometh unto the father but by me.*' I know that the world teaches there are many ways to Heaven. That is one of the devil's biggest lies. There is only *one* way to Heaven, and that's through Jesus Christ, God's Son."

"So what do I have to do?" He raised his hands and

Joseph was glad to see he wasn't shaking anymore. "Because, it's not like I can go to church or anything."

"You don't need to, Maverick. There's only one thing you need to do, and that's turn to God. Repent. Ask Him to wash away your sins. Ask Him to save you. If you truly want to become His child, He will receive you."

"His child?"

Joseph nodded and flipped a page to another passage. "*But as many as received him, to them gave he power to become the sons of God, even to them that believe on his name.*"

"But I thought that Jesus was God's *only* son."

"I think that's why the Bible distinguishes Jesus by saying He's 'the only *begotten* Son of God'."

"I see."

"But your heart must be pure in seeking Him."

"Pure?"

"You have to mean what you say. From the heart."

"Okay. Do I need to pray or something? Can you help me?"

Joseph nodded. "Sure." He bowed his head. "Dear *Gott*, I come to You right now on behalf of my friend, Maverick. *Gott,* I know that You love him and that You love me. Maverick says that he wants to be saved. He's seen what hell is like and he doesn't want to go there—"

"Sure don't." Maverick agreed.

"Maverick, just ask *Gott* to save you now."

"Okay." He bowed his head. "God, I know I've done a lot of bad things in my life, and I'm sorry for doin' those things. But if what Jonah says is true and I *can* be saved, I ask that You will save me. I want to become Your child. Please wash my sins away. Please give me the everlasting life that Jonah just read about. I believe in Your Son, Jesus who died for me. Amen."

Joseph nodded.

"Is that it?"

"That's it, if you spoke those words from your heart."

"I sure did."

"*Gut*." Joseph smiled.

"So, just like that. I'm going to Heaven?"

Joseph's grin widened. "Just like that."

Maverick jumped up with a smile that could blind a man. "Woo hoo! I'm going to Heaven!" He hollered. "I'm going to Heaven!"

Joseph smiled and nodded and tears sprung to his eyes. "Yes, you are. We are."

"I am too." A voice from one of the neighboring bunks said.

"Ricardo? Is that you?" Joseph asked.

"Yes. I pray for Jesus save me too," Ricardo said in his broken English.

"Praise the Lord," Joseph said.

"Yes, praise the Lord!" Maverick shouted. "I'm glad we're in the same cell, because I'm going to give you a big bear hug right now."

Joseph chuckled. Maverick's excitement was contagious. "Okay." He hugged his burly friend.

"Shut up! We're trying to sleep here!" An angry voice came from one of the other cells.

Joseph put his finger to his lips. "We should probably try to get some sleep now."

"You're right," Maverick whispered. "But I think I might just be too excited to sleep now."

TWENTY-SEVEN

Alex pinned a thoughtful look on Maverick as their buddy group sat at a table in the recreation area. "Hey man, why don't you ask the Big Guy in the Sky to get you out of the death penalty? He's still in the business of miracles, right Jonah?"

Joseph nodded. "Far as I know."

Maverick shook his head. "No way, man. I've got a one-way ticket to Heaven. If I stay here any longer, I might mess it up."

"You can't mess it up," Joseph insisted.

"I can't?" Maverick's mouth fell open.

"*How* would you mess it up?"

"By doing something dumb. What if I lose my temper and let out a string of curse words? Or what if someone makes me mad and I take him out?"

"That is the beauty of *Gott's* saving grace, Maverick. It is God that saves you and it is God that *keeps* you saved. No man can pluck you from His hand. That means you. Once you are born again into God's family, there is no way to be unborn."

"So I can do *anything* and still be saved? That doesn't sound right."

"Maverick, did you grow up with your folks?"

"Yeah, but my dad died when I was twelve." He frowned.

"When you did something that went against what he said, when you disobeyed him, what happened?"

"He pulled his leather belt out of his pants and whooped my backside. I hated that." He rubbed his rump as though still feeling the sting of his father's chastisement.

"You are God's child now. If you're doing something that you know is wrong, something that goes directly against His word, guess what?"

"He's going to spank me?" He grinned mischievously.

Joseph nodded. "Like all good parents, He expects His children to behave. When they don't, He doesn't let them get away with it."

"Oh. I don't know if I want a whoopin' from God." He grimaced.

Alex slapped Maverick on the back, clearly amused by this conversation. If he had a bag of popcorn, he'd likely be delighted.

Joseph hoped Alex was getting more than just amusement from this conversation. "The good thing about being God's child is that He is merciful. Unlike our earthly parents, He can see our heart and the motives behind what we do. And He's not going to discipline you for something you *didn't* do."

"Well, that's good to know."

"Another thing. When God saved you, did He say you were receiving everlasting life or temporary life?"

"Everlasting life."

"When does everlasting life end?"

"Uh, never?"

"That's right. So if you *could* do something to lose it, that would mean that you'd have to become unborn, spiritually speaking. You'd have to be able to pluck yourself out of God's hand. *And* you'd have to somehow make everlasting life temporary. On top of all that, you'd be calling God a liar."

"Wow, that's pretty amazing." Maverick smiled.

"It is, isn't it? Being a child of God comes with some really great fringe benefits, wouldn't you say?"

He nodded. "Yep. All this and Heaven too."

Joseph chuckled. It seemed like it wouldn't mean that much, being confined in a prison. But he had more joy now than he'd had in a long time and he was sure and certain it had to do with leading Maverick, and apparently Ricardo, to Christ. If he could do this for the rest of his life, he was sure this peace in his heart would never wane.

If only their friend Alex would see his need for Christ as well. He'd need to keep praying for him.

Looking at Maverick, there was no doubt that this man—destined for imminent death—had more joy than many that were walking around free on the outside. And that joy was something that no one could take away.

God certainly was good.

The moment he had some alone time, Joseph bowed his head and prayed. "Thank You, *Gott*. Thank You for putting me here in this place, at this time. You knew I needed to be here. You've seen this coming all along. I'm sorry for not trusting You, Lord. I'm sorry for thinking You've abandoned me."

Tears shined in Maverick's eyes as the correctional officers waited for him. His brawny arms wrapped Joseph in a fierce bear hug. "Jonah, thanks for everything, man."

Joseph swallowed the emotion in his throat,

knowing this was the last time he'd see his friend Maverick alive this side of eternity. "I'll miss you."

"Only for a short time." His eyes shown with confidence. "I'll see you on the other side, right?"

Joseph nodded. "Yes, you will."

"Hey, I had another dream last night. Same as my first one. But instead of walking to my doom with fear, I had a smile on my face. Jonah, I'm going to Heaven!"

He easily caught his enthusiasm. "Yes, you are, my friend."

Joseph watched as his friend was escorted out of their wing of the facility. Maverick's broad grin and thumbs-up would be something he'd remember for the remainder of his life, he was certain.

TWENTY-EIGHT

It had seemed that since Maverick's departure two weeks ago and Alex's release yesterday, Joseph felt an extra sense of loneliness. He still had four months to go for his early release and he prayed that nothing would happen to prevent it.

At least his friend Ricardo was still here, and was now his 'celly' as they called it. He and Ricardo had daily Bible studies, although his friend's Bible was in Spanish since he understood it better. Their time in God's Word was the highlight of their day and Joseph encouraged Ricardo to continue on once he was gone. There was nothing like God's Word to bring comfort to a downtrodden soul.

Ricardo had informed him that he'd been writing back and forth to his family in Mexico. His parents had discouraged the studies, but one of his sisters had privately sent a letter to him telling about her conversion to

Christianity. They had both rejoiced in her salvation. Joseph knew that was the boost Ricardo needed to keep on sharing his newfound faith in Christ. He'd need to remember to pray for his friend once he was released.

⁂

Chaplain Hal approached Joseph after the chapel service on Sunday afternoon. "Jonah, I know you are going through a difficult time. I can tell that being in here has taken a toll on you."

"It wasn't easy losing Maverick, although I know he's in a much better place now."

"That's right. I feel for you. I really saw a change in Maverick in the short time he'd been saved. Don't ever forget how God has used you in this place."

"I won't. I'm sure that's why he placed me here. But I'm so ready to get out and move on with my life."

"We must remember that God's timing is perfect."

Joseph tapped his fingers on his thigh. "I know. I keep reminding myself of that."

"Jonah, have you considered asking God for a miracle? To move on your behalf?"

"Do you think God could get me out of here even sooner than I'd hoped?"

"Oh, Brother, He can do much more than that. He can do more than what we ask or think. Don't be afraid to ask for the moon—He might just give it to you."

"Well, better than the moon would be to see my father again. But I'm afraid he's likely passed on by now." The probable reality of that thought threatened to bring him even lower. But he did his best not to dwell on things he had no control over.

"Pour your heart out to God, Jonah. He is always listening."

He thought of Azalea. Oh, how he'd love to see her again. "Do you think He'd give me a chance with a billionaire's daughter?" He asked the question in jest, but the chaplain seemed to take it seriously.

"A billionaire's daughter?" Hal's brow shot up.

"Yes, sir." He nodded. "Frankly, I couldn't care less whether she has a million dollars or none at all. None of that has ever mattered to me. But I've fallen in love with her. I thought she was the one, but…" He shook his head. "I don't blame her. Who would want to marry someone who's been accused of rape? And from what I've heard, I'll carry around the title of 'sexual offender' my entire life. I'll most likely never have a chance at a relationship with *anybody* again."

Something sparkled in the man's eye, as though he harbored a delicious secret. "How big is your God, Jonah?"

He shrugged. "Pretty big, I reckon."

"Well, let's just put it this way. God owns the cattle on a thousand hills. His Word states that He delights in giving His children gifts. If He is your Father, that means you.

"A billionaire and a wife may seem beyond your reach, but when you view things from God's perspective, a billion dollars is as a few grains of sand on a hundred beaches. He owns it all. And the Bible says that the king's heart is in the hand of the Lord. If he can turn a king's heart, he can certainly turn a woman's."

"Wow, I guess I'd never thought of it that way."

"Besides, do you think it's fair to prejudge someone just because they have money in the bank? A billionaire is a human being too."

"You're right." Joseph noted the inmates filing out and he snatched his Bible from the chair he'd sat in during the service.

"I'm not saying that it's God's will for you to marry a billionaire's daughter. I don't know what God's will is for your future. But I do know that you may ask Him. The worst He can say is no, right? And if He does say no, you can trust that is His will and that He has something else planned for you. Likely something better than you have planned for yourself."

"Wow, okay. Yeah, you're right. Thank you, Chaplain. You have no idea how much I needed to hear that today."

The chaplain smiled and pointed to the ceiling. "God knew."

"Time is up." A correctional officer approached his cell.

Joseph sat up. "What? What do you mean?"

"Congratulations, Jonah. You've been released early on good behavior."

His mouth dropped open and he shot a look at Ricardo. "You're serious? Because if you're joking, that's not even funny."

"I'm totally serious. We just need to go up to the administration office and sign some papers, get you your release clothes and personal belongings if you have any. Then you're free to go." The correctional officer eyed him. "You've been praying or something?"

"I sure have." Joseph could hardly believe the man's words. *Thank you, God!*

"There's someone who'd like to meet with you."

He frowned. "Who?"

"Governor Hanson."

He'd heard the name on the news before.

"Me? Why?" What on earth would the governor want to meet with him for? It didn't make sense.

"I'm sure he'll let you know."

Joseph wracked his brain. For the life of him, he couldn't figure out why the governor would want to meet with him. He wasn't in more trouble, was he? If that were the case, why was he being set free? *Guide me, Lord. I don't know what's going on but I know You do.*

"Will you give me a minute? I'd like to speak with Ricardo."

"Sure. But don't take too long."

Joseph nodded. He walked to Ricardo after the officer stepped out of the room, and placed a hand on his shoulder. "You keep studying your Bible, okay? I'll be praying for you and I'll write you too."

"Gracias, Jonah." Ricardo embraced him.

"God will be with you. Never hesitate to call on Him."

Ricardo nodded. "I will pray for you too."

"I appreciate that, friend. Look me up when you get out."

"I will." He grinned.

TWENTY-NINE

*J*oseph tapped his fingers on his jeans and held his breath as the fancy car he rode in pulled up to an expansive mansion. He didn't wait for the driver to open his door, but stepped out on his own. He held a small bag of belongings, along with his Bible, in one hand.

"Wow." He stared up at the grandiose estate. *What do you have planned for me now, God?*

"Go on up to the door and speak through the intercom."

"Okay." He hadn't learned what an intercom was until he went to prison. Once again, he silently thanked God to be out of that place.

He walked to the entrance of the mansion and pushed a button on the intercom. "I'm Jonah Millerton. I was told the governor wanted to see me."

"One moment please," a male voice sounded through the speaker.

He stepped back and waited just for a moment before the door opened to him.

"Right this way, please." A man in a suit gestured him inside. Joseph followed him as he led the way to a beautiful room off the side of the foyer. "Have a seat. Governor Hanson will be with you shortly."

Not even a moment later, he was joined by a man who was dressed more casually, yet still distinguished, than the one who'd escorted him into the room.

"I'm Andrew Hanson." He extended his hand.

Joseph shook the governor's hand. "Jonah Millerton."

The man gestured toward a chair. "Have a seat, won't you?"

Joseph nodded and quietly did as instructed, although his nerves were on a Ferris wheel.

"Thank you for coming, Jonah. I bet you're wondering why you're here."

"Yes, sir."

"One of my aides, Mr. Valdez, recommended you."

"Me? For what? I'm sorry, I don't follow." Joseph wracked his brain. Who was Mr. Valdez anyway?

"He said you can understand dreams."

Joseph shrugged. "Sometimes. But it's only because God shows me what they mean."

"Would you be willing to hear me out? I've been

having this same dream over and over again. It's the strangest thing. I can't shake it no matter what I do."

"I can listen but no guarantees. If God chooses to reveal the meaning to me, that's up to Him."

"I understand. All I ask is that you listen."

"Sure."

"Thank you." He sighed.

"Wait. You said Valdez? What's his first name?"

"Uh…Alex?"

Now Alex, he knew. If he was the same one. *Dreams.* Yeah, that had to be him. He'd known all about Maverick's fateful dream. "Wow. Small world."

"Sure is. Now, about my dream…"

"I'm all ears." *Lord, please give me understanding like you have in the past.*

&

Joseph frowned at the governor. "I'm afraid I don't have good news for you."

"Go ahead, Jonah. I didn't ask for good news, I'd just like to know the meaning of my dreams. If you know, please share it with me."

"Okay. Well, the entire Midwest is going to have some terrible weather. The storms are going to decimate the corn production and it will affect the entire country."

"Oh, no."

Joseph blew out a breath. "I told you it was bad."

"What can I do? Is there anything I can do?"

"Well, you can put extra corn away but it'll never be enough to feed the entire country."

"Say on."

"The worst of the foul weather won't be for a few years, but it won't be the weather that causes the total desolation."

"What will it be then?"

"Insects or Parasites."

"Parasites?"

"Yeah. They'll destroy everything and there will be nothing you can do about it."

"Can't I just spray an insecticide on it?"

"Nope. The strain that is coming will have built up a resistance to all commercial insecticides and herbicides. Not to mention that stuff causes cancer and all sorts of other health issues for the consumer."

Governor Hanson folded his hands together. "So, what kind of destruction are we talking about here? Will there be a famine in the entire country?"

"That depends."

"On what?"

"On what course of action you take."

"What do you advise?"

"It's hard to tell for the long haul. But since it seems like this will only affect the corn crops, I suggest growing an alternative crop. You'll need to warn the farmers."

"Like what?"

"Well, I'd suggest doing a soil test to see what crops—other than corn—the acreage will tolerate. If farmers heed the warning and grow other crops, the country will be able to wade through the bad years. If they won't heed the warning, well, let's just say those who did will have a whole slew of hungry families on their doorstep."

"Replacing established crops can be very expensive. I'm not sure the farmers will be willing to do that."

"Then they'll be risking their very lives."

"What if you're wrong?"

"Believe me. In this case I wish I were. But I'm not. This will happen whether people choose to believe it or not."

"Oh, man. I don't know if I'm ready to handle something like this."

"You have a few years yet. And you can hire someone to manage it for you. It has to be someone who will be responsible—a person you can trust."

"Will you take the position? You have more knowledge in this than anyone I've ever met."

"Me? You trust me for this? In case you didn't realize it, I *just* came from prison. Straight from prison. I'm not sure I'm your man."

"You're definitely my man, Jonah. I have it on good authority that you were falsely accused."

"What?"

Governor Hanson grinned. "That's the word on the street. And if it's true, you're entitled to press charges for false imprisonment."

"I've chosen to forgive. I didn't relish my time in prison and I'd never wish a prison sentence on anyone."

"You really are something else. By the way, do you have a place to stay?"

"No. Like I said, I just came from prison. I was planning to look into that."

"Stay here."

"Here? In the Governor's Mansion?"

"If you're going to be my assistant, I can't very well have you living at the Rescue Mission. Can I?"

Joseph shrugged.

"Really, Jonah, I insist." He smiled. "I'm also offering you a sign-on bonus along with your first six months' salary in advance."

Joseph swallowed. "How much is that?"

212

"Let's just say you'll be able to afford a nice down payment on a house, a car, and whatever else you'll be needing."

"Oh, wow. I don't know what to say. Thank you." After making twenty-five cents an hour while working in prison, this offer felt like a million dollars.

"You're welcome. But I really should be thanking you."

"I'm sorry but I can't take any credit for this. It's God and God alone."

"Well, then I guess I'll have to thank Him too."

THIRTY

*J*oseph jumped from the plush chaise in his room and set his Bible on the small table next to it. He pulled the door open to answer whomever had knocked from the other side.

"Mr. Millerton, the governor would like you to join him for dinner." A petite uniformed woman stood on the other side of his door.

He frowned down at the jeans, polo shirt, and white tennis shoes he wore that seemed to have stamped on them 'straight from prison'. "I don't have proper attire."

"He said to come as you are. It will be a casual affair." She smiled.

"Okay, thank you."

"The meal will be served in twenty minutes."

Joseph nodded. "Thank you."

"Thank you for joining me. This will be somewhat of a business dinner. I hope you don't mind. We'll convene with a meeting in my office after dinner, unless you have other plans."

"Uh, no. I have no immediate plans."

"Good. Won't you have a seat?" Governor Hanson gestured to a chair at the table, where a fancy place setting, along with stemware filled with water, had been attentively placed.

"Thank you." He'd never sat at such a fancy table, although the china reminded him of the set *Mamm* had kept in her cupboards. On very special occasions, she'd take it out and use it.

"I've also invited another guest, one of my closest advisors. I'm excited for you two to meet. I feel you'd have quite a bit in common."

Joseph frowned, wondering if he was referring to Alex. But no, he'd said 'meet' as though the man were a stranger.

The governor glanced down at his watch. "He said he was running a little late. He should be along shortly."

"Great." Joseph took a sip of his water.

"Do your accommodations suit you?"

He felt like laughing. After almost a year and a half in prison, sleeping in a car would have been wonderful. "Yes, sir. My room is perfect. Thank you."

"Do you have any questions about anything?"

"I do, actually. I've been thinking about something. Well, you brought me here, and Alex is here too…" He shrugged. "Do you make a habit of hiring former prisoners? Not that I'm complaining or anything. I just find it interesting."

"I can see how one would think that's strange." The governor chuckled. "Let's just say that I'm a firm believer in second chances. I've always considered myself a pretty good judge of character. Alex was a former employee and he messed up, but he's a good guy. I'm not perfect, nor do I expect others to be. And as for you, well, I'm hoping to find a great asset in you. If one of my friends recommends someone, I don't take that lightly. I'm confident you will meet or exceed my expectations and conquer the challenges ahead of us."

A couple of voices echoed through the entrance to the kitchen.

"It appears our guest has arrived." Governor Hanson smiled and rose from his chair.

Joseph was unsure what to do, so he took his cue from the governor and stood as well.

As soon as his guest walked through the door, Joseph grinned. "Chaplain Hal?"

"Jonah! What a pleasant surprise. I had no idea." The man stepped forward and embraced him heartily.

"I take it you two already know each other?" The governor smiled.

"We do. And, Jonah, I'd like to introduce you to someone else." Chaplain Hal said with a twinkle in his eye. He stepped back into the room he'd emerged from with a young woman on his arm. "My daughter."

A freight truck running him over couldn't have impacted him more. Joseph looked back and forth from the young woman to Chaplain Hal. "Azalea?"

It felt like the wind had been knocked out of him. His heartbeat quickened. The room began to spin. He might just fall flat on his face at any moment.

"I'm sorry. I can't do this." Joseph rushed past all of them and hurried to the front door, desperate for some fresh air. *Azalea is here? And she's Chaplain Hal's daughter?*

This wasn't a dream—it was a nightmare.

Why, God? As soon as I regain my bearings, You throw me for another loop. I don't understand this. What are You doing? My heart can't take much more, Lord.

"Jonah?" Azalea's voice called from behind.

No, not now. He squeezed his eyes shut. "Please. Just leave me." He didn't dare turn around.

"I had no idea you'd be here. Really. I thought you were still—"

"In prison?" He shook his head. "Where I should be, right?"

"Jonah…" She sighed. "I want to apologize. Dad said that he believes you were innocent this whole time."

"He does?"

"Yes."

"And what about you, Azalea? You still believe I'm guilty, huh?"

"I'm still trying to process all this. Honestly, I don't know what to think. With all my heart, I *want* to believe that you're innocent."

"But you don't," he said flatly.

He felt her hand touch his shoulder.

"Please. Turn around. Look at me." Her voice trembled as she spoke the words.

He shook his head. "I don't know if I can."

She moved to stand in front of him and lifted his chin so their eyes met. "I still love you." A tear slipped down her cheek as she spoke the words.

He ached to pull her into his arms. "No, you don't," he said roughly and stepped back from her. "Love is built on trust. You don't even trust me. You *can't* trust me, Azalea."

"I'm trying."

"Trying isn't enough." He moved to the side. "Now, if you'll excuse me, I must go inside."

With that, he strode back toward the entrance.

"Jonah! Please. Don't go." Azalea's desperate cry was practically his undoing.

He couldn't stand this a moment longer. He squeezed his eyes shut and took a deep breath. Then he abruptly spun around and marched toward Azalea. Without a word, he wrapped one hand around her waist and the other behind her head and pulled her close. Before she could complete her gasp, his mouth pressed firmly against hers and he gave her the kiss he'd kept bottled up for nearly the past year and a half.

She responded with equal passion and sighed when they broke away from each other.

"Marry me." Joseph's eyes searched hers. If she *did* love him, as she said, agreeing would be the ultimate declaration of trust.

"I…"

He met her hesitation with another breathless kiss.

"Marry me?"

She nodded, as though convincing herself it was the right thing to do, then nodded again with a smile the size of Indianapolis. "Okay. Yes, Jonah. I'll marry you." Her teeth tugged her bottom lip inward.

"Really?" A cautious hope kindled in his heart. His eyes examined hers for a hint of doubt, of reticence. "You're *really* saying yes?"

"Yes." Tears shined in her eyes. "Yes, Jonah. I'm *really* saying yes."

He closed his eyes and tossed his head back. "Thank You, God."

"Let's go inside and talk to my father." She grasped his hand and started toward the door.

"Wait…do you think…?" He shook his head. "I don't know…"

"Jonah, my father loves you."

"He does?"

"Yes. He will welcome you into our family with open arms. He would come home from his prison chaplain duties and talk about you. He'd talk about what a good man you are."

"Wow, I…"

"Come on." She tugged his hand again.

"Okay, if you're sure."

"I've never been more sure about anything."

THIRTY-ONE

"I have an urgent phone call to attend to." The governor motioned to his office. "If you'll excuse me, I'm going to step out for a few moments."

Joseph, Hal, and Azalea all nodded in understanding.

"I still can't believe that *you're* Azalea's father." Joseph leaned forward on the couch and shook his head. He forked a bite of the delicious cheesecake he'd been served and savored the creamy texture.

Chaplain Hal smiled, sipping his coffee. "The one and only."

"So this whole time..." Joseph's mouth went slack. "Wow." There was no doubt in his mind now that God had all this planned from the beginning.

"When we spoke the first time, I didn't know it was you. It wasn't until Azalea opened up to me that I realized that you and her boyfriend were one and the same."

"But you…? I don't understand. You know what I've been accused of. How can you trust me with your daughter?" He glanced at Azalea sitting next to him, who seemed to be quietly listening. Either that or she was entranced by the magnificent dessert they'd been served. He winked and she smiled back.

"From what Azalea's told me about you, and from what you've told me and the behavior I've seen from you while in prison, combined with my knowledge of Miranda Brandenburg, let's just say I'd take your word over hers any day."

Joseph's forehead wrinkled. "But I thought your families were friends?"

"In a very loose sense of the word. We've never been close, although, if Miranda would get her way, we'd be quite a bit closer."

Azalea gasped. "What do you mean, Dad?"

"Do you remember after your mother passed away?"

Azalea nodded and set her empty dessert plate on the coffee table.

Hal continued. "The Brandenburgs had brought over a couple of meals. Well, let's just say that I had a feeling that she was offering more than just condolences."

Azalea's hand flew to her chest. "Really?"

"She never made a pass at me, like she did Jonah, but

her body language told me that she was…available." He shook his head.

"That's terrible." She reached over and squeezed her father's hand.

"I never had any concrete evidence other than the way she eyed me and her tone of voice. And I tried my best to ignore it. Just tried to steer clear of her."

"I can't believe that, Dad. I never had any idea."

Joseph lightly rubbed Azalea's back, hoping the motion would calm her.

Her father shrugged. "Well, it's not really something I wanted to shout from the balcony. And poor Fred."

Hal blew out a breath. "But when I met Jonah in prison and he'd declared his innocence, I didn't automatically dismiss it like I usually do. Something inside told me to keep an open mind. And then, when I learned that it was Miranda who'd been the one to file the charges, well, I tended to believe Jonah's words even more. And every time we met, I became more and more convinced of his innocence."

"But couldn't you have spoken up for him? Got him an appeal or something?" Azalea leaned forward on the couch.

He shook his head. "I didn't have any clear evidence. I'm still trying to decide whether I should have a talk with Fred. The situation is rather embarrassing. And I'd hate to lose his friendship. But he probably should know about his wife's shenanigans."

Joseph sighed. "There was most likely nothing you could do anyway. Besides, I'm confident that it was the Lord who put me in that prison, not Mrs. Brandenburg."

"You're right. Didn't you say that you were able to lead a few prisoners to Christ?"

"A couple, yeah." Joseph smiled and nodded. "That's the best feeling in the world."

"Isn't it? Knowing you've made a difference for eternity…" Hal's grin widened.

"Not that I want to go back there or anything."

Azalea linked her arm with his, pulled him close and kissed his cheek. "No way. I'm not letting you go again for anything."

THIRTY-TWO

Three months later

"Come on." Azalea stood from the couch in her father's great room and reached for Joseph's hands.

He pretended to allow her to pull him up, but instead pulled her down into his lap. He brought her close and kissed her thoroughly. "I don't think I want to go anywhere," he mumbled.

"You need clothes for our honeymoon. I'm taking you shopping."

He frowned. "Shopping? Really?"

"I'd thought you'd be happy to spend the day with me." She gave a faux pout.

"Yes, but shopping?"

"I've been dying to see you in a pair of Wranglers and a western shirt." The warmth of her hand on his chest through his shirt could get him to say yes to almost anything. "And we can go someplace special for lunch."

"Special?"

"Or wherever you'd like to go." She shrugged.

"How about Chick-Fil-A or Cracker Barrel?"

"I'm game. Let's go?"

He held her stare for several seconds, longing for the day he could share all his love with her. "Your wish is my command."

Joseph strode out of the dressing room, sporting the clothing Azalea had picked out for him. A pair of jeans that fit him just right, a plaid button-up long-sleeve shirt, and comfy leather cowboy boots. His shirt size had upgraded to a large due to the time he spent working out in prison. To his delight, Azalea had commented on how she appreciated the extra bulk. And he admitted that he didn't mind it much himself either. He turned around at Azalea's prompting so she could examine his getup.

She whistled. "Wow, Jonah Millerton. Cowboy looks *really* good on you." She shook her head.

The corner of his mouth lifted at her unabashed assessment. "You think so?"

"No. I *know* so. I'm going to have the handsomest husband this side of the Mississippi."

He chuckled. "Lying is a sin, Azalea."

"No lie." The light sparkled in her eyes. "But you're missing something."

He watched as she walked over to a table display and lifted a cowboy hat to check the size.

She sauntered back and placed it on his head. "There. Does that fit you or do you need another size?"

He moved the hat slightly to make sure there wasn't too much wiggle room between his head and the inside comfort band. The last thing he needed was for his hat to go flying off when he and Azalea were out riding. "No, this fits just fine. But I already have a hat."

"Just like a girl can never have too many books, a cowboy can never have too many hats."

"Books? I thought it was shoes?" He chuckled.

"What can I say? I love books." She shrugged.

"Okay, if you say so."

"I do." She winked. "Oh, wait. You need a belt buckle too." She hurried to a carousel that held several and picked one with a horse on it.

He shook his head. "I think those have to be earned at a rodeo or something, don't they?"

"No fiancé of mine is going to get bucked off a raging bull and have his back broken. We can buy one."

He shrugged. "If it's good enough for you, I guess it's good enough for me."

"It is. Alright, try on the other outfits so I can see them on you."

"Then can we leave?"

She laughed, then mimicked his pouting tone. "You really don't like shopping, do you?"

"No, but I do like eating." He raised his brows.

"I think I've figured that out already." She teasingly tipped his hat up and he was tempted to take her in his arms and kiss her then and there in the middle of the store.

She then playfully put her hand on his chest and pushed him back into the dressing room. He'd love nothing more than to pull her in there with him, but remembered his sense of propriety.

"Alright, I'll just…" He closed the door, lest he lose his head, determined to finish the task at hand. He heard Azalea giggle from the other side of the dressing room door and smiled to himself. She knew *exactly* how she affected him.

Jah, as his former Amish self would say, they made a *wonderful gut* couple for sure and for certain.

THIRTY-THREE

*N*ever in a million years would Joseph have pictured his wedding day like this. He'd always seen this day as a day of rejoicing with his family—with *Dat* and his older brothers, with Dinah, with Benji. He attempted to loosen the bowtie at his neck to no avail.

Bittersweet emotions rose in his chest, but quickly dissipated the moment he glimpsed his beloved standing at the back of the church in her long white gown. He had a new family now—Azalea and her father.

Azalea's smile spoke of the love in her heart as she waltzed up the aisle on her father's arm. The instant their eyes met, Joseph's knees felt like they might give way. Was he really about to marry the woman of his dreams?

Oh, God. I don't deserve this. I don't deserve her. I

don't want to disappoint her. I don't want to fail her. Please help me to be the husband she needs. Help me to lead her in Your ways and cherish every moment I have with her.

As she joined him, she leaned forward and whispered in his ear. "You look so handsome." Her eyes shined with love.

He could hardly believe that in a few moments, they'd walk out of this building as husband and wife—together. Forever.

"How's married life treating you, Jonah?" Governor Hanson's knowing countenance told Joseph that he already knew the answer before he asked. Joseph had been pleased to find a friend and confidant in the governor.

"Better than I deserve, for sure. It's wonderful, Andrew." He grinned. "You know, back when I was younger, my father had talked about my mother and how someday I'd find *the one*. Well, I've definitely found her. Azalea is my soulmate."

"That reminds me of the verse in the Song of Solomon. *I have found him whom my soul loveth.* That's what my wife said to me the day I proposed to her."

"Really?" Joseph smiled. "That's pretty cool."

"Yeah. Again, congratulations."

"Thanks."

"Now, about work…"

"I knew we were getting around to that subject." Joseph chuckled. "Everything's looking good so far. Of course, we won't know much until the reports from the other farms come in. But if they follow the advice we gave them, it shouldn't be too bad."

"The forecast is calling for stormy weather." The governor grimaced.

"Yep. This is just the beginning."

"But we'll be fine, right?"

Joseph wanted to give the governor reassurance, but the outcome was up to God. "I'm confident we will be."

"Good."

"We've harvested as much as we can this season. We'll have to leverage the distribution wisely because we won't bring in any more until next year."

"I understand."

"Let's just trust God with this."

"We will. That's why I hired you, Jonah. Thank you for agreeing. I really don't know where I'd be—where the state would be—if you'd declined my offer. I have no doubt that God brought you to my doorstep." He stood up and shook his hand.

"Me either, Andrew. This was definitely a 'God thing,' as Azalea would say."

"You know, it's funny. When you first came here, I had no idea what to expect. Let's just say that I've been pleasantly surprised. It's strange. You're like the younger brother I never had."

Joseph's head snapped up. "What?"

"I mean it, Jonah. If I could choose a younger brother, it'd be you."

Joseph blew out a breath, doing his best to conceal his emotions. He pressed his lips together. "Thank you for saying that, Andrew. You have *no idea* how much that means to me."

THIRTY-FOUR

"Jonah, come quickly. Look at this. It looks like it's starting." The governor called him over and held out a half-shucked corn cob. "Alex told me you've had experience saving plants?"

"Some, yeah. But there could be a number of things wrong." Joseph frowned at the splotches on the corn. "Wait a minute. I think I might know what this is."

"You might?"

"Yes, and I *might* know how to stop the destruction. If we can stop it, we may not need to plant other crops. When I was at home, something like this threatened to take over our crops. On a whim, I concocted a solution and sprayed it on the plants. Amazingly enough, the disease disappeared and the plants grew healthy."

"What was it?"

"My sister's special homemade soap, water, and vinegar."

"Do you know how to make the soap?"

He frowned, but then recalled the day he'd made soap with Dinah. He'd been at a curious age so he'd asked a lot of questions. She'd patiently answered each one. Thank God he'd helped her that day. And this was God's doing, wasn't it? *Jah, it's all God.*

He thought about the herbs she'd used—anti-parasitic she'd called one of them. But it wasn't just one herb, it was a special combination. "*Jah*, I think so. But getting ahold of some of the ingredients might be tricky."

He'd never even imagined that on that one day he'd made soap with Dinah, God was actually preparing him for this day, over a decade into the future.

"You just let me know what you need and I'll get it for you."

"I'll need to make up a test batch. If it's successful in combatting the disease, we can make it in quantity."

"That sounds good."

"Alright. Let's get on it." He pulled out the notebook and pen he kept in his pocket and scribbled down several items. "I'll need these things along with soap making equipment. I can start as soon as I get it."

"Sounds good. How long after application will you know if it works?"

"About twenty-four hours. But if it does the job,

we're going to need to assemble a crew to make this stuff."

"I've got all the man power you'll need. Just say the word and they'll be at your disposal."

"Thank you, Andrew."

"No, thank you, Jonah. I truly do not know what I'd do without you."

Joseph surveyed the rows of corn he'd sprayed yesterday. "It worked! Praise God, it worked!"

"Great! Woo hoo!" Andrew embraced him with a hearty bear hug. "We need to make this in bulk to sell. When people come to us to purchase grain, we'll also sell them *The Millerton Cure*. That way, they can learn to be self-sufficient. At least, it will take care of them until they run out. When they do, they'll return and buy more of the cure."

Joseph chuckled. "The Millerton Cure, huh? I think I like it."

"You have got to patent this formula, Jonah. I know all the people to contact and the channels to go through. When you've done that, we'll set up a website so buyers can pre-order—although they'll need to pick it up here."

"I'm not sure about all this. I don't want any special glory."

"I don't know about glory, but you're certain to become a millionaire. At least."

He frowned. "Really?" A millionaire?

"Jonah, what you've got here is gold. You've done so much for me. I want to do this for you. I want to help you. If anyone deserves to succeed, it's you."

He shook his head. He wasn't sure how deserving he was, but he knew that God at brought him to this moment. "Wow. Okay, thank you."

⁓

Joseph stood next to Governor Hanson as he addressed the production workers.

"Okay, the distribution center is officially open for business. The news stations have made it public. I expect our first customers to come rolling in at any time." Andrew glanced down at his watch and smiled with confidence.

"Won't that be chaotic?" One of the lead men asked.

"No, the way Jonah has things set up is brilliant." The governor assured. "It's only by appointment. We've directed them here first, then those who request

The Millerton Cure will be directed to the warehouse where they can pick that up."

"But are you sure we'll have enough?"

"As far as the corn goes, there's no guarantee of that. It'll be first come, first served. Exact amounts will be measured out per household and will vary according to age. But Jonah's solution will assure that their own crops don't fail."

Another worker raised his hand. "What happens if someone comes without an appointment?"

He gestured toward Joseph. "You'll direct them to Jonah. I'm confident he'll be able to handle any situations that arise."

The foreman grinned. "It sounds like you have it all figured out then."

"I'm expecting a smooth operation. And I know it will be with Jonah overseeing it."

THIRTY-FIVE

$\mathcal{J}$oseph eyed the group of men as they approached with one of the workers. Indeed, they were Amish, as he suspected. He blew out a breath. It had been so long since he'd beheld a person from his native culture. He'd expected more, since the Amish community closest to them was less than an hour away, but these were the first to arrive.

"Jonah, these men have come without an appointment. They're asking for quite a bit. Governor Hanson said to direct them to you."

"Thank you, John. I'll handle it." Joseph nodded to dismiss him, then turned to the men. "How may I help you?"

"We have come from Canaan in Switzerland County."

His head snapped up at the mention of his former home. He noticed their distinct Swiss Dutch accent and examined each of the men, mentally counting them again. Seven. Sure enough, these were his older brothers.

At that moment, it dawned on him. His brothers didn't recognize the non-Amish version of Joseph. Certainly, his name change helped with that, but he guessed it was mostly because of his brawny build and facial hair that concealed his true identity. He'd been just a kid when he'd been forced from his home.

"You don't have an appointment. I don't think we can accommodate you," he answered roughly. "You should have followed procedure."

"Please. We didn't know. We do not have a television. We weren't told an appointment was necessary."

He rubbed his beard, then crossed his arms over his chest. "You've come to scope out our operation, haven't you?"

"What do you mean?" Judah raked a hand through his hair. "No. We just want to buy some corn and some of The Millerton Cure solution."

Joseph admitted that the name rolling off of his brother's tongue did sound satisfying. He shook his head. "I don't think so."

"No, please. We have no intention of harm. We are just seven brothers who have come to purchase corn for our families. Our father and brother and sister are at home, along with our wives and children."

In one fell swoop, his brothers bent their knees before him, bowing their heads.

In a split second, his dream from a decade prior flashed before his eyes. *This* is what the dream had meant! *Thank you for showing me, Lord.*

He cleared his throat and they stood again. "If you do indeed have another brother, why didn't he come with you? Sounds suspicious to me."

"He had to stay home with our father. You see, we had another brother but he passed. He meant everything to our father. The youngest is the next closest to him."

"Is he ailing?"

"*Nee*, his health is decent. But *Dat* would never approve of bringing Benjamin along. Our younger brother means the world to our father."

Joseph frowned and pulled out his cell phone. "John, I need Alex to come up here."

His brothers spoke to each other in Swiss Dutch, believing he couldn't understand their words. They were clearly worried.

Alex came and stood at Joseph's side and grinned. "Yes, boss?" The fact that he called him 'boss' had sort of been a joke between the two of them.

Joseph kept a straight face. "Take one of these men and detain him."

243

"What? We haven't even done anything!" Simeon protested and Joseph nodded to him.

Alex grasped Simeon's arm.

"As soon as you produce this younger brother that you say you have, I'll believe your story. Until then, we'll detain this one."

He dismissed Alex with a nod, then watched him escort Simeon out of their sight.

The brothers once again spoke amongst themselves in Swiss Dutch. "Surely this is because of our past sin. God is punishing us." Levi had said.

Joseph clear his throat. "I'll call up John and send you back with corn for your families. The sooner you return with your brother, the sooner the other one can go free."

Judah couldn't dissuade the worry in his thoughts as their driver pulled the van onto their property. How on earth were they going to convince *Dat* to allow Benjamin to go back with them?

But they *had to* return. If retrieving Simeon weren't enough to persuade *Dat*, returning the money had to be. Somehow, the money they'd taken to pay for the corn came home with them. They hadn't discovered it until they were nearly home. He had no idea how it could've happened. He distinctly remembered paying the man himself. If Mr. Millerton hadn't been convinced they were spies already, surely this would confirm it. Either that, or he'd think they were thieves.

"Who's going to share the news with *Dat*?" Reuben asked, yanking him out of his reverie.

Judah sighed as each of his brothers looked around, then pinned their gaze on him. "Why me?" But he already knew.

"You're the one he respects the most. You know how to deal with him best."

He shook his head. "*Nee*, I doubt that."

"Still."

Judah expelled a breath. "I'm going to dread this, you know that, right?"

"We have confidence in you, *bruder*." Dan patted his shoulder.

"*Jah*. Whatever." Judah rolled his eyes, then eyed Reuben. "You know, *you* should be the one doing this. *You're* the oldest."

"Maybe, but *Dat* will listen to you."

He couldn't argue with Reuben because he knew he was right. If *Dat* would listen to anyone, it was him.

This task wouldn't be any easier than when they'd

shared the news of Joseph's demise. And *that* had almost killed their father. But this wasn't about a death or losing a son. It was just a trip into another area of the state. No big deal. Surely, it wouldn't present a problem.

He hoped. And prayed.

"*Dat*," Judah frowned. "We need to go back and take Benjamin with us."

His father's hands began to shake along with his entire body and he sobbed uncontrollably. He didn't expect his father's emotional outburst, but he should have figured.

"I've already lost Joseph! I *will not* lose Benjamin too!" Their father's chest heaved and they feared a heart attack might send him to his grave then and there. "You will not take him."

"But Simeon's being detained. That would mean he must stay there." Levi frowned and glanced at Judah.

"So be it. I *will not* lose Rachel's only son! I refuse to! He's all I have left of her." His voice shook with a sob.

If only their father had loved them with the same passion he'd felt toward his second wife's two children. Had he not loved *their* mother at all? If he had, perhaps Joseph would still be here on this property. His brothers wouldn't have thought ill of him because he was

Father's favorite. But this was how it was. And by the look of it, how it would always be. They'd never be equals in their father's eyes.

But none of that really mattered anymore. They'd done both Joseph and their father wrong. And now it was clear that God was working against them—Judah knew it.

He wasn't sure how all this would work out, but if they didn't bring Simeon back home, that would be another brother lost—permanently. Because, the man who'd demanded he stay meant business. And he had power that none of them could possess.

It was nothing short of a miracle that they'd been able to return with food. Perhaps he was mistaken. Perhaps God was on their side.

THIRTY-SIX

*J*oseph sat out on the balcony, thinking of the day's events. He'd nearly lost his composure after his brothers left. He could hardly believe that Simeon was still here awaiting his brothers' return. He'd given strict instructions that he be treated with kindness, noting that he wasn't an actual prisoner, just a detainee. His brother's experience would be nothing like his own prison sentence had been.

His wife came through the sliding glass doors. Oh, how she could brighten up his day with just her presence.

"Azalea, babe." He reached for his wife's hand and pulled her down beside him on the loveseat.

"What is it, Jonah?" She caressed his trimmed beard and gazed into his eyes. "Have you been crying?"

"There's something I need to share with you." He swallowed. "It's about my past."

"Your Amish past?"

"Yes." He blew out a breath. "There's so much to tell. I don't know where to begin."

"Start at the beginning?" She intertwined her fingers with his.

"Okay. I won't tell you everything, just the parts you need to know."

"Whatever you want to share with me is fine." She squeezed his hand. "I can tell a burden's been sitting on your shoulders."

He nodded. "Do you remember those men who came?"

"Jonah, we've had hundreds of men come."

"You're right. Do you remember the guy I put in jail?"

"You mean the one who was with the men who you thought lied to you?"

"*Nee*. They weren't lying."

"I don't understand."

"Those men are my brothers."

"You sent one of your brothers to jail?" She moved away. "Jonah, I don't understand. That's not like you."

"I gave instructions for them to treat him well." He sighed. "Trust me. They *all* deserve much worse."

"What do you mean?"

"Growing up, my older brothers hated me. One day,

they decided to do something about it." He shook his head, trying his best not to let tears form in his eyes. "Azalea, I believe they intended to kill me and they thought they did."

"Jonah, that's terrible!" She moved close and rubbed his back. "What happened?"

"They beat me to a pulp and threw me into a garbage receptacle. If God hadn't sent someone along to rescue me, I'm certain my brothers would have gotten their wish."

"I can't believe that. Why?"

"They were actually my half-brothers. We had different mothers. Dad love mine and Benjamin's mom more than anything. I guess he didn't have the same feelings for his first wife." He shrugged. "I think they were jealous. I was always closest to our father. I think they wished they had that same relationship. Now that I look back on it, I can kind of understand their animosity toward me. Dad treated me better than everyone else."

"I'm failing to see how that was *your* fault. It's not like you'd deny your father's affection."

"I know. But sometimes I wonder if maybe there was something I could have done to make things better, you know?"

"Don't blame yourself. You are a good man. If you

were anything like you are now, I can see why your father favored you." She lifted his hand to her lips and kissed it. "I know I do."

"I thought they'd done me wrong, and it's true they did. But now…" He shook his head. "Azalea, I can see that it's all been God. God has been with me every step of the way. Leading me. Guiding me. And I think that if my brothers had not done that—dumped me at the right place, at the right time—then I wouldn't be here with you. We wouldn't be enjoying the blessings that we are now. I wouldn't have been able to help Governor Hanson. It's like God put me here on purpose."

"So, was it worth it?"

He gazed into the eyes of his beloved. "A thousand times over. Not that I enjoyed being beaten by my brothers or being in prison or being away from you or my father…" Tears pricked his eyes. "Azalea, not only is my father alive but I might get to see him again! I can't believe it."

"I'm happy for you, Jonah." She kissed his lips.

"By the way, now that I'm sharing my past with you, you might as well know that my name isn't Jonah Millerton."

"What?" She moved back.

"Well, it is now. But it's not the name I was born with."

"Jonah!" She lightly slapped his knee.

He shrugged. "I didn't want my brothers to be able to locate me. And I wanted to start a new life with a clean slate."

"So, what *is* your real name?"

"Joseph. Joseph King."

"Hmm…" She studied his face. "Yeah, I guess Joseph King suits you too. But you'll always be Jonah to me. I fell in love with Jonah Millerton."

"That's fine by me, Mrs. Millerton." He winked.

"By the way…" She pulled something out of her pocket and placed it in his hand.

He frowned down at the white plastic device that reminded him of a kazoo, trying to decipher what it was. He stared at her in confusion. "What is it?"

Her smile spread across her entire face. "It's a secret message." He could tell by the twinkle in her eye that she was teasing him.

He thrust his palms upward. "I don't get it."

She laughed. "You are so cute." She took the device from his hands. "See this?" She pointed to two small lines.

"Yeah?"

"It means that you are a daddy." Her eyes sparkled with pleasure.

"Wait. What?"

She bit her lip and nodded. "You're happy, right?"

"Happy? You mean we're going to have a baby? You're pregnant?"

She nodded.

Inexplicable joy filled his heart. He pulled his wife close and kissed her soundly. "Oh, Azalea. I'm beyond happy."

THIRTY-SEVEN

Several months later...

Judah brought the sprayer into the barn. The conversation he needed to have with his father was sure to be a difficult one, but he couldn't avoid it any longer.

"We're down to the last of the solution, *Dat*. If we don't get more, we'll lose this next crop." Judah's voice was grave. "Our grain supply is almost down to nothing. We have no choice but to go back to Mr. Millerton."

Dat ignored his words. It seems he'd rather pretend that everything was fine than to face the facts.

But Judah knew all too well what the facts were. "We've already butchered half of the herd. If we butcher the other half, we'll have nothing. Without going back, we won't have food for us or the animals to eat or money to live off of. We need to go back to the supplier, *Dat*. We won't survive."

"So go."

"*Dat*…" He exchanged glances with Reuben, his silent partner. He dreaded his next words, which he knew would be met with resistance. "We'll need to take Benjamin along."

"No."

"Then what do you plan to do, *Dat*? If we don't show up with Benjamin, the man will not sell us the solution or any more corn." His jaw clenched.

"Get it elsewhere."

Why did his father have to be so bullheaded? Judah threw down his hat and his hands practically screeched through his hair. "There is nowhere else! There is only *one* supplier for the entire country, *Dat*. Either we buy it from him or we lose everything."

He hated losing patience with his father, but sometimes *Dat* just refused to listen to reason.

His father broke down in tears.

Judah gentled his tone. "*Dat*, I *promise* I will bring Benjamin back home."

His eyes pleaded with Reuben to help him out.

Reuben stepped forward. "If we don't bring Benjamin back, consider my sons your own."

No doubt, his brother hated making such a promise,

but without it they'd lose more than just his sons. Besides, they owed much to his father. They should have been protection for Joseph all those years ago. Apparently, he wasn't the only one who'd been consumed with guilt.

"Fine. Take him. But if I lose him…" *Dat's* voice broke off in a sob.

Judah touched his shoulder, hopefully offering the reassurance his father needed. "You won't lose him. I promise you won't."

God, please let it be so.

Joseph looked up from his clipboard, just as John and Alex approached him. They pointed to a white van.

"Jonah, the brothers of the man you had detained have returned," John said.

"They have?" His brow jumped. "It's about time."

"Yeah, I thought that poor guy might be here indefinitely." Alex chuckled.

"They didn't make an appointment. Again." Joseph frowned.

"With all the commotion that happened last time, they probably forgot," John reasoned.

"They sure aren't making this easy on themselves." He shook his head. "Go ahead and fetch the guy that's detained and bring him up to the house."

"Yes, boss." Alex grinned and Joseph shook his head.

"John, will you see to it that the other men find their way to the house as well."

He nodded, but gave him a strange look. "You're sure?"

"Yep. I'll meet you there." He turned back. "And John?"

"Yes, Jonah?"

"Order a half a dozen pizzas and have them delivered to the house. Just order a variety."

"Sure thing. Whatever you say…"

Joseph grinned, but trepidation bounced through his being. What would his brothers say when they found out his identity?

Reuben glanced over at Judah as they waited for Mr. Millerton. "Why do you suppose he wanted us to come to his house?"

Judah shook his head. "I don't know, but I'm worried." He frowned.

"You told his foreman about the money, right? Do you think he believed you?" Dan asked.

"I don't know. I don't have a good feeling about this." Judah grimaced.

"Well, maybe he'll be pacified when we offer him gifts," Levi interjected.

"I don't know. I know *Dat* meant well, but I'm not sure bringing gifts was the best idea. If the man already thinks were spies…" Dread filled Judah's heart.

"Is this guy really as scary as you say he is?" Benjamin asked.

"Times ten," Zeb said.

"Shh…I think I hear someone coming." Judah whispered. "Don't say anything stupid, brothers."

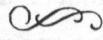

Joseph walked into the great room, where he'd instructed John to leave his brothers.

"I see you finally made it back." He raised a brow.

"Yes. We had a difficult time convincing our father to let Benjamin come along." Judah's frown deepened. Surely he must be nervous.

"And this is your younger brother?" He gestured toward Benjamin. He could hardly believe how much he'd grown. He was practically a man.

Oh, how he felt like wrapping Benji in a big bear hug! But he refrained.

"Yes, that's Benjamin," Judah replied.

Joseph briefly nodded toward his younger brother. "I had some pizza ordered. I hope you're hungry."

Each of his brothers looked at each other. Their astonishment was clearly recognizable.

"Listen, Mr. Millerton. When we went back home, somehow the money we'd brought along the first time went back with us. I'm not sure how that happened. We brought it back, along with money for the corn and solution we plan to purchase this time." Judah rambled on. "And our father insisted that we bring some gifts along. We brought you a quilt that our sister made, along with some pot holders, an Amish doll for your daughter—uh, if you have one, and some soap and jam. We also brought some harnesses and a couple of saddles. We saw that you had some horses."

Joseph simply nodded. "Very well, then. Won't you take a seat at the table? Your other brother should be along shortly."

Joseph noticed that Reuben shared a questioning glance with Judah. Judah lifted his shoulders, then did as Joseph instructed.

"Uh, thank you. How has Simeon been?" Judah asked.

"Don't know. I don't make it my business to visit detainees." Joseph shrugged casually.

At that, Alex ushered Simeon in. All eyes turned to him, most likely to see if he'd been harmed.

"You may have a seat next to your brothers." Joseph nodded curtly to Simeon, then dismissed Alex.

"Do you need anything else, boss?" Alex grinned from the exit.

"Nope. You're free to go. But don't go too far in case I need you." He winked covertly at his friend.

"Yes, boss."

His brothers shared another look with each other and he noticed that Judah blew out a breath. Surely this would be the worst pizza they'd ever eaten. Joseph was unsure if even he would enjoy it with the way his nerves skittered.

THIRTY-EIGHT

"Thank you for dinner, but we should probably be getting back to our father," Judah said graciously as he stood from the table. "He will be worried if we tarry too long. Especially with Benjamin along."

Joseph stood as well. "How is your father? Is he in good health?"

"He is."

"Tell him thank you for the gifts he sent. And thank your sister as well for the nice things she made." Joseph nodded.

"I will."

He watched as each of his brothers filed out of the house, then radioed John as soon as the door closed.

"Hey, John, do me a favor…" he spoke into the radio.

Judah and his brothers finished loading up the corn and The Millerton Cure they'd purchased. He sighed, glad to be finally returning to his place of refuge. This trip had been stressful, but seemed to turn out okay for the most part.

"Alright, everyone. It's time to go. Load up." He ushered his brothers into the van. "I don't know about you all, but I am more than ready to go home."

"Me too," Levi said. "That guy freaks me out."

"Ah, he's okay, I guess," Judah said.

"Well, I'm just glad I'm not at his mercy anymore," Simeon grunted.

"Where's the driver?" Dan leaned forward in the seat.

"Who knows? Didn't you tell him we were ready to go, Judah?" Reuben asked.

"*Jah*. I did."

"Oh no. Don't look now, but that man's coming toward the van," Benjamin said.

"Which man?" Judah turned around just as Mr. Millerton approached with two men at his side. *He doesn't look happy. Oh, no.*

"May I help you?" Judah stepped forward, doing his

best to sound confident although he was not feeling it at all.

"Something is missing from my house," Mr. Millerton frowned.

"Your house? What? What's missing?"

"My wife's favorite painting."

"I'm sorry, Mr. Millerton. But my brothers and I are not thieves. I assure you that none of us has taken your painting." At least he *hoped* none of his brothers would do something so foolish. "Right, brothers?"

Each one of them shook their head, insisting they hadn't taken it.

"Then you won't mind while my men search through your things." Mr. Millerton insisted.

"By all means…" Judah gestured toward the van. "Why don't you guys come out while the men search?"

His brothers did as suggested.

"Here it is, boss!" The man Mr. Millerton had called Alex held up the painting.

Judah's mouth went slack. "I don't know how that happened." He looked at each of his brothers and they all shook their heads.

"Where was it?" Reuben asked.

"In this backpack." Alex held up Benjamin's travel bag.

"Benjamin?" Judah's brow shot up.

"I promise, I didn't take it!" Fear shot to his baby brother's eyes.

"Lock him up!" Mr. Millerton frowned and motioned to his men.

They immediately took Benjamin by the arms and led him toward the house.

"No!" Judah cried. "Please! Don't take Benjamin. Our father will not survive."

Mr. Millerton seemed to ignore them, continuing to the house behind the men who held Benjamin captive.

"I promised him my sons if Benjamin doesn't return. He has to come home with us!" Reuben insisted. "Judah, we have to do something."

Judah ran after Mr. Millerton and dropped to his knees in front of him, along with the rest of his brothers. "Take me instead! Please. I beg you! I beg you! Take me." He couldn't stop his tears from flowing.

THIRTY-NINE

Joseph motioned to Alex and John and had them escort his brothers to the great room once again. He disappeared into his room. He couldn't stand it any longer. How his heart yearned for his family!

"God, I need Your direction here." He cried until he didn't think he could stand being away from his brothers a moment longer.

He hurried to the bathroom and washed his face, erasing all evidence of tears.

When he thought he was emotionally able, he reentered the great room.

"John, Alex, I'll handle this from here. You're free to go." He nodded to his friends.

"Sure, boss." Alex grinned as he stepped out the door.

Joseph waited for a moment, then went and locked the door.

"Listen, Mr. Millerton—"

He held up his hand to silence Judah.

He looked to each of his brothers, and then his eyes finally settled on Benjamin.

"I am your brother, Joseph." He annunciated each word so there would be no confusion. He looked to each one again. "I am your brother, Joseph. The one you thought you killed. The one you beat up and threw into a dumpster."

Each one of his brothers, Benjamin excluded, looked at each other as fear took hold of them.

"You don't need to be afraid. I mean you no harm." He broke down in tears.

He moved closer to his youngest brother, who stood across the room. "Benjamin, Benji, it's me. Your brother, Joseph."

"Joey?" His brother carefully studied his face.

He chuckled, remembering his little brother's name for him. "Yes, Joey."

His brother then practically ran to him. Joseph threw his arms around him and wrapped him in a fierce hug. "I've missed you so much, Benji."

"I missed you too. I cried so much when you…" He brushed away a tear. "I can't wait to tell *Dat*. He will be so happy! He hasn't had joy since you left."

His other brothers came near and he hugged each

one. "We're sorry, Joseph. Please, forgive us for what we've done to you."

He stepped back and swiped at a tear. Each of his brothers had clearly been bawling too. He shook his head.

"You guys meant to harm me, but God turned it all into something good. Look how He has helped me to preserve our state, our country. If you hadn't done what you did, I might not be here. Your families might very well be starving."

"But we wronged you."

"I know. I've forgiven you. Now, we can move on. Together. As a family." Joseph smiled. "I want you to go back and tell *Dat* that I'm alive. Tell him that I want you all to move up here. He can sell his land and buy some here. I did some research online. There is a Swiss Amish community nearby and you can join there. There is plenty of good land in these parts. Tell *Dat* he can own twice of what he owns now. I have enough money to purchase property for each of your families, if you cannot afford it."

"Joseph…" Judah's mouth hung open. "You're sure?"

"Yes. I insist. I want Father close the rest of his days." He tapped his hand on his pant leg. "I will send trucks and trailers along to haul the cattle, sheep, goats, and horses. I'll also send a moving van with hired movers so *Dat* doesn't have to do any of the work."

"Okay. Well, it looks like it's all settled then. We're moving." Judah glanced at each of their brothers and Joseph could sense the excitement in their smiles.

He couldn't help the feeling of satisfaction that welled up inside. He couldn't wait to share the news with Azalea.

Joseph grasped Azalea's hand and brought her to his side. "Azalea, meet my brothers. Reuben, Judah, Simeon, Levi, Ash, Dan, Gad, Zeb, and Benji."

She stepped forward and shook each of their hands. "It's nice to finally meet some of Jonah's family."

"This is my *fraa*, Azalea. As you can see, we have a *boppli* due soon." He grinned.

His brothers squirmed just a bit and he remembered that it wasn't the Amish way to announce pregnancies. Of course, he'd known so little about that sort of thing when he'd left, he could probably claim innocence.

"Congratulations. It's nice to meet you too, Azalea." Judah grinned and shared a knowing look with Joseph.

Joseph watched the road in anticipation. They'd be here any moment.

Azalea came up behind him and lightly massaged his shoulders. "Jonah, honey, why don't you come sit down? You've been watching out that window for the last half hour."

"I can't help it, babe. *Dat* will be here any minute! It's been nearly ten years since I've seen him." He couldn't wipe the smile off his face if he tried. "They're here!" He walked to the door. "Come."

Joseph watched the van pull into the driveway and roll to a stop. The moment *Dat* stepped out of the vehicle and spotted him, his father ran toward him. "Joseph, my *sohn*! You are alive! My *sohn* is alive." *Dat* grasped the back of his shirt at his shoulders and wept.

"I've missed you so much!" Joseph didn't know how long they stood there embracing each other, but he couldn't have imagined a greater reunion. *Dat* had come!

EPILOGUE

Three months later...

Joseph had been going back and forth in his mind, but the time to make a decision had come.

He'd never been to many *Englisch* churches, but Azalea had assured him that their church was conservative compared to most modern churches. But that meant little where Amish culture was concerned. To make the jump from not meeting in a house or a barn to meeting in a church building was drastic enough. But to throw in everything else—men and women sitting together, musical instruments on the platform, women with uncovered heads and some even wearing men's trousers, singers, taking up an offering, and a preacher that used a microphone—was downright overwhelming to someone who grew up in a totally different culture. Joseph still remembered the sheer shock he felt the first time he'd attended. He could only imagine what *Dat* would think.

Yet, at the same time, he wanted his family to attend so badly. *Jah*, his first experience had been shocking. But it had also been eye-opening to hear how the preacher spoke with such authority and he loved how the music seemed to speak directly to his soul. It wasn't as though he'd be asking them to make a lifelong commitment or anything, it was just one service.

"*Dat*, I would be honored if you and the family would attend my baptism on Sunday."

His father frowned. "At an *Englisch* church? *Ach*, Joseph, you know that is not our way."

"Please, Father? It would mean the world to me to have you there." Tears pricked his eyes. How wonderful it would be to worship *Der Herr* with his family again.

"I will think on it, *sohn*."

Joseph reached over and squeezed his father's shoulder. "*Denki, Dat*."

Joseph paced back and forth. He had to get an answer from *Dat*. He'd prayed half the night, pleading with the Lord. But he knew that getting a devout Amish man to attend an *Englisch* church was akin to getting a wild mustang to pull a buggy. Both were highly unlikely.

He took a deep breath and whispered one last plea. His father walked beside him and once again remorse filled him as he thought of the wasted years they could have had together. But they hadn't really been wasted—at least not on his part—they'd been redeemed. And now, here they were walking side-by-side in the field like they had when Joseph was a boy. God had been gracious in not only allowing his father to live, but in giving Joseph time with him. For all he'd known, *Dat* could have already passed on. *Jah, Der Herr* had once again displayed His loving kindness.

"*Dat*, about church this Sunday? Do you have an answer for me? I'd like you and the family to join Azalea and me."

His father frowned. "*Englisch* church?"

"*Jah*, it's *Englisch*. I'm getting baptized."

"For you, my *sohn*, we will go this one time. For you, Joseph." He patted his hand.

Thank You, Lord! "*Denki, Dat.* You don't know how much this means to me."

"It means even more to me." Joseph didn't miss the tears in his father's eyes.

He then leaned close and whispered in his ear. "I have a secret."

His father looked back at him, and curiosity twinkled in his eye. "*Jah?*"

"You're going to be a *Grossdawdi* yet again." Joseph grinned. "*Mei fraa* is in the *familye* way."

"*Ach*, Joseph. That *is wunderbaar gut* news!" A hint of mischief glinted in his face. "I know a secret too."

Joseph grinned. How good it was to have his father near. "Say on."

"There's a certain widower in our new Amish district that has approached me about your *schweschder*. *Gut* man. Has five *kinner*. I think it's a right *gut* fit."

Joy welled in Joseph's heart. "What does Dinah say?"

"You know your *schweschder*. She's quiet and keeps things to herself most times. But she seems to be agreeable to it. I've seen her glance his way more than once."

"*Ach, Dat. Gott* is *gut*, ain't so?"

"*Jah, sehr gut*, Joseph."

He reached over and squeezed his father's shoulder. "*Ich liebe die, Dat.* I am happy *Der Herr* made you *mei vatter.*"

He knew that Amish didn't often say words of endearment, and although Joseph was no longer Amish, he knew a part of him always would be. But he wanted *Dat* to hear the words he'd held in his heart. He wanted *Dat* to know in word and in deed that he'd be loved until the day he passed on to glory to be with *Der Herr*.

Joseph leaned toward Azalea, who gently rocked little Jacob in her arms, and whispered, "I didn't know your father would be preaching today."

She smiled back at him. "Neither did I."

He glanced down the pew and at the one behind him, thrilled and amazed to see his entire family present, wives and children included. Their gazes were riveted on the platform.

Dinah glanced his way. Oh, how he loved to see a smile on his sister's face. Their reunion had been a blessing for all of them.

His father-in-law stood behind the pulpit and began his exposition of the Word of God. Joseph hung on every word.

Lord, please speak to our hearts today.

Joseph lifted his head slightly at the conclusion of the service. Not just one, but all seven of his older brothers now knelt at the altar. Had God given them a change of heart? He prayed with all his being that it would be so.

What would it be like to have real fellowship with his brothers? What would it be like for them to actually treat him as a brother? What would it be like to not only be brothers physically, but spiritually as well? His heart soared at the thought.

God had already wrought so many miracles in his life, it seemed. He wouldn't dare ask for another one, but he *would* pray for God's will to be done. God's will was always best.

Simeon approached Joseph after the service. "We're all having dinner at *Dat's* and we'd like you and your family to join us."

Azalea came close and squeezed Joseph's hand. He smiled at his brother. "We'd be honored, Simeon."

"May I bring something?" Azalea asked.

"Nope. Just yourselves," Judah chimed in behind Simeon.

Joseph's eyes misted. "Thank you. We'll be looking forward to it."

Jacob King sat on his porch swing, gently propelling it forward with the ball of his foot. He turned to Joseph beside him. "I think all of God's children will get to the end of their lives and step into eternity and see how everything they'd gone through on this earth was worth it."

Joseph nodded. "When I think of all that Christ suffered through, I can't help but think that my struggles were nothing by comparison. Those in Christ's time intended Him harm, but it actually resulted in the salvation of mankind."

"Just like the way your brothers intended harm upon you. God has taken what was intended for evil and He turned it into something beautiful. It resulted in saving many from hunger and giving us the family we never would have had otherwise. Joseph, God has been good to us." Jacob took Joseph's hand and cradled it in his own.

Joseph smiled at his beloved father. "Yes. Yes, He has. God's goodness is beyond words."

THE END

Dear Reader,

Thank you for reading *An Amish Honor*. I truly hope it was a blessing.

The Biblical story of Joseph has always been a personal favorite. I love how much Joseph represents Christ. So many things in his life were similar to the life of Christ. It never ceases to amaze me how God continually brings good out of what man intends for evil. In the end, we know that love will conquer all.

Has there ever been a time in your own life when you couldn't see God's hand in what you were going through? Or perhaps you're walking through that fog of uncertainty at present. You can rest assured, if You are God's child, that He is holding you in the palm of His hand. You may not be able to see through the fog, but He sees clearly. Trust His hand.

We have this assurance from God's Word: *For I know the thoughts that I think toward you, saith the LORD, thoughts of peace, and not of evil, to give you an expected end.* And what is that expected end for the child of God? Jesus gives us the answer in John 14:2-3, *In my Father's house are many mansions: if it were not so, I would have told you. I go to prepare a place for you. And if I go and prepare a place for you, I will come again, and receive you unto myself; that where I am, there ye may be also.* Wow, a mansion in our

Father's house and everlasting life with our Beloved! Isn't that amazing?

Rest assured, my friend, that God *will* do what He promises!

Blessings,
J. Spredemann

P.S. If you have a friend who might be struggling in their faith, or, like Maverick, is unsure of their eternal destiny, or who needs to hear a word of encouragement, please share this book with them.

Thanks for reading!

To find out more about J.E.B. Spredemann, join our email list, or purchase other books, please visit us at www.jebspredemann.com. Our books are available in Paperback, eBook, and Audiobook formats. You may also follow J.E.B. Spredemann on Facebook, Pinterest, Twitter, Bookbub, Amazon, and Goodreads.

Questions and comments are always welcome. Feel free to email the author at jebspredemann@gmail.com.

Discussion Questions

1. Although Joseph's father meant well, his actions (that he considered to be love toward Joseph) actually fostered hate in his other children, ultimately causing Joseph harm. Have you ever experienced a situation in which you meant good but it turned out bad?

2. Sibling rivalry can be a very real problem, especially in a mixed family. Have you experienced sibling rivalry in your own life? How did you deal with it?

3. In spite of his brothers' ill will toward him, Joseph chose kindness toward those around him. How can we rise above the negativity in our lives and keep a positive attitude?

4. Joseph knew very little about the *Englisch* culture before it was thrust upon him. How do you think

you would cope if forced to live in a completely foreign culture without friends or family?

5. Do you have a favorite Old Testament Bible story? Which one, and why is it your favorite?

6. At the time they occurred, Joseph had no idea why he went through the trials he did. Have you ever found yourself in a place wondering why?

7. Sometimes trials come for no apparent reason. At other times, they result from our own foolishness. Have you ever considered how your actions might affect other people?

8. We can allow trials to either tear us apart or strengthen us. How can we keep from growing bitter while going through a trial? (Please see Isaiah 26:3 KJV)

9. Bit by bit, Joseph was able to eventually see how God was working in his life. Even at his death, he still hadn't seen the completed picture. Can you look back on the trials in your life and see how God had been working all along?

10. Joseph was confident with sharing the truth of God's love and salvation with his friends. Do you have boldness when it comes to sharing your faith?

11. In the end, Joseph was able to see how it was worth it all. As believers in Christ, we will eventually be able to see our difficult circumstances as blessings as well. How can we encourage our brothers and sisters in Christ to 'count it all joy' when life presents difficulties?

12. As children of God, we have a hope that this world knows not of. How can we share this hope with them?

13. Joseph had several spiritual mentors throughout his life. Do you have a spiritual mentor? Have you ever mentored someone spiritually?

14. Joseph's life (in the Biblical account) exemplifies how we, as Christians, should live and has been considered by many to be the closest comparison to Christ. What lessons can you take from Joseph's life and his Godly character and apply it to your own life?

A SPECIAL THANK YOU

I'd like to take this time to thank everyone that had any involvement in this book and its production, including my Mom and Dad, who have always been supportive of my writing, my longsuffering Family—especially my handsome, encouraging Hubby, my former-Amish friends who have helped immensely in my understanding of the Amish ways, my supportive Pastor and Church family, my Proofreaders, my Editor, my CIA Facebook author friends who have been a tremendous help, my wonderful Readers who buy, read, offer great input, and leave encouraging reviews and emails, my awesome Street Team who, I'm confident, will 'Sprede the Word' about my books! And last, but certainly not least, I'd like to thank my **_Precious LORD and SAVIOUR JESUS CHRIST_**, for without Him, none of this would have been possible!